BABY
SPECIES INTERVENTION
#6609

Prequel to the Species Intervention Series

J.K. Accinni

EK Publishing
Lakewood Ranch, FL

This is a work of fiction. Names, characters, places and incidents are either the product of the author's imagination or are used fictitiously, and any resemblance to actual persons, living or dead, business establishments, events, or locales is entirely coincidental.

BABY
SPECIES INTERVENTION #6609
J.K. Accinni

An EK Publishing book published in arrangement with the author, Lakewood Ranch, FL.

ISBN: 978-0-9899769-0-9

Library of Congress Control Number: 2012947136

Other Books by J.K. Accinni:

Echo (Species Intervention #6609, Book 2)

Armageddon Cometh (Species Intervention #6609, Book 3)

Hive (Species Intervention #6609 Book 4)

Evil Among Us (Species Intervention #6609, Book 5)

The One (Species Intervention #6609, Book 6)

Alien Species Intervention Books 1-3

Dedication

I would like to thank my mom, Jane, for her unflagging support. She never once thought to even question my capabilities. I owe so much to my one true love, Wil, whose honest clear sweetness and support gave me something to live up to, and I would like to thank Fate.

I would like to thank the phenomenally talented artists who granted me the rights to their work for my covers, Adam Taylor, England, United Kingdom—*Baby;* Larissa Elise Bergsma, Netherlands—*Echo;* Jonas Jedicke, Berlin, Germany—*Armageddon Cometh* and *The One;* Terry Rogers, Gainesville, Florida—*Hive.*

And lastly, I want to acknowledge my four legged children, Barney, Toby, Molly, Teddy and Echo, and all of my children who are waiting for me over the Rainbow Bridge. They are what bring all the richness and laughter into my life.

NOTE TO READERS: This is a work of fiction and as such, controversial points of view may be written to enhance the reader's experience. The author's goal has been to make the reader think critically and the views expressed do not necessarily reflect those of the author. The author would like, however, to help readers realize what detrimental effects we have created for our wildlife.

Readers, in an effort to make this work as appropriate as possible for the time period in which it takes place, the author has used more formal grammar and not used contractions as readily as we use them today.

Chapter 1

1929

It came to young Netty in her sleep. The first probing finger, an aura glinting under the sleeping eyelids of her brain, unnoticed. She lay under shabby blankets in the primitive bed of her murdered mama, in the tiny remote cabin of a loving childhood. Now, her debilitated physical condition crippled her to the point of numbness. She tossed in her sleep, disturbed by the pain of the injuries that continued to bedevil her, taking unwanted turns with the unseen alien presence which explored her unguarded mind.

The night passed too quickly, as it always does when overwork and fear become your only companions. Rising early, intending to continue the repairs she doggedly hoped to complete, she found herself ignoring the fireplace that begged a spark.

Drawn to the broken door of the cabin, she stared into the quiet woods at the far side of the field, affected by an unfathomable magnetic pull. Nothing moved; familiar maples and oaks were frozen in their leafy majesty. The eerie stillness unaccountably frightened her. She felt goose bumps lift the hairs on her plump work-worn arms. Against her will, she stepped out onto the narrow stoop and down the few steps to head across the fallow field.

Netty trudged around the wild blackberry thickets until she came upon the hint of a faint path; all that remained of the well-worn trail she'd traveled incessantly as a child. The nebulous pathway led her directly through the foreboding woods until she reached a familiar cleft in a rocky outcrop. Looking down at her damaged feet, she saw her open sores blossoming with blood and pus, her inability to stop the infection worrisome. *Why oh why should I make this needless and excruciating foray into the damp morning fog? I cannot spare the time and, God knows, I plainly do not have the strength.*

Only two weeks had passed since she'd made her unexpected escape from the humiliation and abuse she regularly tolerated from the sick bastard she'd married. Was this sudden and strange compulsion to take to the woods a punishment for running away from him? Or did the spirits of the devil invade her in her sleep? Visions of her abusive husband carting her off to the insane asylum at Graystone near their mansion in Norristown convinced her she must continue on. Hoping to discover the meaning of the annoying compulsion that drove her against her will and wisdom, she trudged onward.

Needing a break from the exhausting trek, she rested her feeble body, swiping her thinning, ratty brown hair off her forehead. She contemplated the progress made on her tiny two-room cabin in the last two weeks.

She swallowed, trying vainly to choke back a bitter sob. It had taken a mighty big bucket of blood, pain and trampled illusions to get to this point, but she thought she might now be safe from Robert.

She wondered how a pathetic wretch such as herself had mustered the nerve to leave him despite his powerful ability to intimidate and bend her to his will.

To reassure herself, she touched the small round object pinned to her undergarments underneath her bodice. Strange how the purloined object could give her a quick shot of comfort. She unapologetically brushed a sudden flush of shame aside. She'd taken the little treasure in a futile and petty attempt at revenge. A sour laugh slipped out, alongside the knowledge that nothing in her sadly wasted life could compensate her for the newly discovered and premeditated betrayal by her older husband. Her head still echoed with the hateful revelations made by him a mere fifteen days ago.

Steeling herself as she rested, she tried again to concentrate on the progress made at the cabin in the last few days. Was it only two weeks since she'd first arrived back on Lily Pond Road? *Why call it a road?* she thought ruefully. *Should it not be called Lily Pond Rut*

Field, as progress has clearly failed to reach this far from town, even after all this time?

The journey had almost defeated her. Her feet bled from numerous injuries incurred on her long trek from the big city back to Sussex County. Her house slippers hadn't been her first choice for the trek, but her husband's unexpected return as she'd searched his precious library had left her no choice. Abundantly sure she could no longer bear more of his scorn, violence and mocking laughter, she ran. And she ran. And she ran, until her hobbled condition forced her to collapse upon Lily Pond Road. The very road that told her the beloved home of her childhood could be found around the next bend.

As she'd approached the dilapidated cabin, she'd noticed the roof had sagged. Could she figure out how to repair it on her own? She could surely try. *Well, maybe not,* she thought, quickly becoming discouraged as she took in the ravaged fence, broken windows and crushed mailbox, her family name still faintly legible.

A wave of despair and loneliness had hit her hard. Her lovely mama and poor papa were gone. Papa to the flu when she'd turned fifteen and her mama murdered, shortly after her very own storybook wedding on her seventeenth birthday. She bitterly remembered the halfhearted search for the culprit. Sheriff Hudson had eventually decided it had been the work of one of the gypsies that frequently passed through the countryside, begging for handouts.

She well understood that the peasantry mattered little to the social and economic fabric of the town. They wielded no influence and were of little consequence. The sheriff had actually told her that something like this was bound to happen with her pretty mama living all the way out in the boondocks with no man of her own to keep an eye on her. Even the surprisingly cooperative intervention of her new and prominent lawyer-husband had had remarkably little effect on the investigation, such as it had been. Impotence had silenced her as the investigation had quickly and quietly concluded.

Two weeks ago, she'd discovered that Mr. Woods, Papa's boss and Mama's longtime childhood friend had died. A special friend to her since she'd been a toddler, she remembered his actions at her wedding with love. He'd pulled her aside, telling her how beautiful she'd always be to him as he slipped a small but plump purse into her hands. He'd whispered to her to keep it to herself, saying every bride needed a little something for herself in case of emergency. Not that she'd actually have an emergency, good heavens no, look who she'd just married.

Yeah, look who I had just married. The bile in her throat rose as she thought of him. Robert Doyle, the only son of a large and prosperous Irish family in town. His five older sisters were known far and wide for the thoroughbred horses they raised for the races in Saratoga. They sported expensive wardrobes, lavish parties and haughty demands. How had a fancy man like him even discovered her? *Oh yes, Robert*, she thought bitterly. *So handsome, so formal, so rich . . .* He'd surely had his choice of all the young, educated, fancy town ladies. Why had he picked her, Jeannette Elizabeth Smith?

As Netty picked burrs off her papa's moth-eaten trousers, which she'd found shoved beneath her parents' old bed in the cabin, her memory drifted back to happier times.

She could almost feel the wetness on her arm as she remembered the frequency of annoying raindrops that had leaked down on her head in the simple mission-style classroom of her schoolhouse. It had sat a full five dusty and hilly miles from her home. She'd never been anything but an average student, daydreaming her way through class until she could return home to check on the latest batch of rescued bunnies, or the baby bird knocked out of its nest by greedy nest mates. She'd attended school until her thirteenth birthday; old enough to start pulling her weight around the farm fulltime. Her education had stopped there, although she'd continued to read the storybooks her mother had provided from her own precious stores. Her heart warmed as she remembered the education derived from the magic of stories painted by so many ingenious authors.

Although her papa had said she was smart and awfully pretty, she'd been passed over time and again by the eligible young men in Sussex County. And by some not so eligible. She'd often been judged too young, too poor. When Robert had started courting, she'd found herself non-responsive, unfamiliar with the mysterious intricacies of flirtation. The fact that he'd been forty years old to her sixteen naturally intimidated her.

Her mama had rapidly convinced her to make an effort with her appearance when she'd realized his attentions merited serious consideration. All reservations about Netty's tender age flew out the window. Gone, her papa's hand-me-down trousers. In their stead, she wore the lovely new dresses her mama had stitched, spending hours working late into the night as she herself lay curled up on her straw mat next to the toasty fieldstone hearth of the blackened kitchen fireplace.

She'd gently stroked the silky fur of her favorite doggies, tiny Nip and one-eyed Molly, as her mama worked the unfamiliar fabrics that had been provided by Mr. Woods. Her mama and Mr. Woods had been intent on making sure Netty didn't let this very sudden opportunity slip by, both convinced it might be her only chance to get off the farm; a fortuitous rescue from the ignoble plight of spinsterhood. God knew if another chance would come along with Netty's perpetual habit of spending every free moment in the woods or wrapped up in her latest creature rescue.

Mrs. Smith had longed for her baby girl to avoid many of her own early mistakes, which had led to their current circumstances. Mr. Smith had been a good, God-fearing man, but Mrs. Smith had wanted Netty to have the wonder of true love, just as she herself had once experienced. She especially wanted her away from the farm; a wistful hope for an easier life of comfort and security. Every mother in the county plotted to secure the best suitors for their daughters, and Mr. Woods had vouched for Robert himself. After all, Robert's favorable legal wrangling with Mr. Woods' extensive farm holdings had kept him lucratively employed for years.

Netty had felt quite content on the farm with her parents. Mr. Woods often stopped by to consult Papa on farm business. He never failed to bring special treats for all of them: sweets for her, bolts of good, strong sack cloth for Mama, books for them both and horrible-smelling tobacco for Papa. She remembered with delight her mama's blushes and rare girlish giggles as Mr. Woods surprised her with the occasional store-bought piece of finery, not understanding her papa's silence, long after Mr. Woods had departed.

Far behind the tiny cabin stood a well-constructed outbuilding previously used to store winter firewood, seeds for the next year's plantings and the trellises for her mother's bean crop. After much lobbying to Mr. Woods as a child, she'd finally persuaded him to agree, amid much laughter and hearty encouragement, to her turning it into her very own animal hospital. For it was Mr. Woods who'd owned the shed, along with the surrounding two thousand acres, as well as the little cabin Netty and her mama lived in. Netty thought Mr. Woods was probably her best friend.

So, it had been with the jubilant blessings of her parents and Mr. Woods that Netty had accepted Robert Doyle's proposal of marriage, although she'd waited in vain for the elusive feelings described by her mama as true love.

Netty forced her thoughts to return to her present dilemma. She'd spent every minute since arriving at the cabin moving gingerly on her damaged feet: cleaning cobwebs, shooing away harmless black snakes and field mice, stocking in some meager supplies and linens, collecting firewood to buffer her from the biting cold evenings and attempting to repair the dilapidated furnishings remaining in the cabin.

Upon reflection, she now understood why Mr. Woods had failed to rent the cabin after her mother's death. Robert had wasted no time in taunting her with the secret he'd hidden from her since Mr. Woods' sad passing. Too late, it was now perfectly clear why he'd married her.

Netty tried to stand, wanting to get off the cold damp ground of the woods. Struggling, she doubled over with nausea as cramps painfully contracted her abdomen from the memory of the events that had forced her to flee her marital home in Norristown.

Her escape had come on the heels of the expected appointment of

Robert as the new county magistrate. *How nice for him*, she thought bitterly. She wondered how he'd explain her conspicuous absence at his induction and the subsequent ball he'd planned at Sunnydale, their ten-thousand-square-foot Renaissance Revival mansion. Thinking about his lavish spending, she no longer wondered where the money came from. His country lawyer fees couldn't possibly cover the household expenses, not with the house staff, the office staff and Robert's outrageous lifestyle. A lifestyle he'd hidden from her during their courtship. Not that she cared. As long as she didn't have to participate in his social affairs, she'd been able to remain safely out of sight and mind.

She'd also developed an aversion to the smell of the harsh spirits imbibed to excess by Robert and his cronies during their constant late night meetings in the carriage house behind the mansion. Meetings that had inevitably turned into drunken brawls, often drawing the attention of local law enforcement; who would then do what? *Well . . . join in, of course; so much for enforcing the law.* Did the police ever bother to wonder where the prohibited alcohol had come from?

The thought unexpectedly reminded her that she was down to the last few silver coins Mr. Woods had pressed into her hands at her wedding. Yes, she'd encountered many rainy days in her marriage, but none as nasty or desperate as this. Relief briefly flooded her mind, amazed by her unexpected wisdom when she'd heeded his wise advice, retaining the coins until she was truly desperate. And yet the cabin needed so much more to become fully habitable. She felt pressured to make every coin stretch three times as far.

Late yesterday afternoon her feet had given out, forcing her to rest as they refused to heal from her self-destructive trek from Norristown. As she soaked her feet, reclining against the unforgiving headboard of her parents' primitive bed, the harsh, roughly-planed wood dug into her plump shoulders and she imagined rainbow colors in the periphery of her vision. An aura, gone in a flash, it left behind an unmistakable urge to visit the woods. She fought the compulsion, recognizing the time and effort involved. Her exhaustion begged her not to go. Clearly, a visit must wait. Chores, dinner and desperately needed sleep came before a break or jaunt into the wood.

So here she was, a day later. She slowly breathed out a ponderous sigh, knowing she needed to get a move on if she wanted to climb to her secret sanctuary and still have time to absorb joyous memories of her childhood. Nightfall could come quickly in the woods.

Netty again tried to get to her feet, this time with more success, and set off. She squeezed her large frame into the painfully tight cleft in the rocky hillside, choosing to avoid the wider expanse of the longer route. She was overwhelmingly aware of how her slender figure had ballooned in the few years since her sham of a marriage. She wondered if perhaps it had been a subconscious defensive move to dissuade Robert's occasional drunken late night forays into her third floor bedroom. It had been there that he'd chosen to indulge his malicious need to remind her of her powerlessness. Just as he'd done on their wedding night.

The evening had started out full of promise, her innocence perfectly clear, even as her mama tried to prepare her by tentatively discussing the rituals between a man and woman in love. Not able to grasp the significance of the talks, she came away convinced that her wedding night would prove to be mysterious and wonderful, capturing the feelings of the true love her mama described to her. Delivered to the bridal suite, she'd prepared for Robert's arrival, the canopy bed so sumptuous she dare not sit on it.

Readying herself for her husband, she'd donned the new nightgown her mama had painstakingly stitched for her. She'd never held anything this elegant, with its delicate lace and silky translucence. As she brushed her long brown hair, thick and gleaming, she'd casually wondered what was keeping Robert. He'd pulled away from her after the ceremony to welcome his boisterous friends, barely speaking to her apart from an occasional dance. The crowded room had consisted mainly of strangers. Robert's sisters formally congratulated her, but had quickly moved on to other party guests. She understood his need to play host to his friends and business associates, although the unfamiliar smell of spirits she'd detected on his breath as they danced had left her confused and nervous.

Time passed quickly and, before long, she'd nodded off on the petite water silk divan in the far corner of the bedroom. She'd startled awake as Robert stumbled into the room, locking the door behind him. It was very late and her innocent eagerness had dissipated with her grogginess from not having properly slept. As she yawned herself awake, she'd softly inquired as to his whereabouts.

Robert had stood in front of her, lightly swaying on his feet as he regarded her with what she could only describe as a sneer. Without warning, he'd backhanded her across the face; the strike so powerful that she'd fallen from the divan. He'd turned toward the bed, then turned back as if he'd suddenly thought better of it. He'd hauled her to her feet, his face transformed into something unfamiliar and strange. Pausing his hand in midair, he'd reached out and slowly, so gently, caressed her bodice. Before she could react, he'd viciously gripped the bodice and yanked it down, fully exposing her trembling nakedness. Lust had filled his eyes as he painfully bit down on her nipple, causing her to scream in shock and pain.

He'd backhanded her again, whispering ominously, "You stupid strumpet, do not ever question me again." With further disdain, he'd then pushed her to the floor. Struggling to pull down his trousers, he'd mounted her from behind, slamming into her tender virgin flesh. His big hands wrapped themselves around her throat, cutting off her air. Disgusting sounds emanated from him, reminiscent of hogs fighting in their pig slop. By the time he'd finished, her screams had lessened to shocked and gulping whimpers. She'd cowered defenselessly on the floor as he'd grunted his way to the bed and collapsed, falling into a deep stupor.

Netty lay stunned, her beautiful fantasy dissolving into the reality of the burning pain and blood between her legs. She felt numbness on her face. Reaching up, she felt her nose and realized Robert had broken it. Hot tears streamed down her swelling face as she slowly made her way to the wash bowl. She'd tenderly blotted at her thighs with clean linen, wincing at the ruin of her nose in the looking glass above the stand. Gathering up the remnants of her lovely nightgown, she'd achingly pressed the ruined gift to her heart. *Oh, Mama, please come take me home.*

Netty had then slipped into her robe and carefully crept to the bottom corner of the bed where she'd silently curled up, praying that the morn would come quickly. Suddenly, Robert had tossed in his sleep. His foot shot out from under the comforter, slamming into her bottom as he viciously kicked her off the bed.

"Country trash does not sleep in my bed." He'd snorted drunkenly as he contemptuously rolled over to sleep. She'd crept over to the tiny divan, careful not to soil the beautiful silk with her blood.

Netty had woken to the warmth of the sun streaming into the room, announcing a steamy summer morning on the wane. Her body ached all over. Her nose had swollen to twice its size and was canted to the side. She glanced at the bed, discovering her husband's absence with relief.

Running quickly to the door, she'd found it locked. Puzzled, her heart thumping wildly, she'd known it was not a good sign. As she gingerly dressed and packed, hoping to escape back to the cabin and her mama, she'd heard noises in the hallway. After some fumbling with the lock, the door slammed back against the wall with a bang. Her husband had strolled into the room accompanied by his manservant, Eli, and several older housemaids. Upon his order they'd grabbed her then plunked her down on a mahogany slipper chair. Amid her protests, she'd noticed Eli carried a large pair of sewing shears in his rough meaty hands.

Robert had proceeded to lay out the rules for her. She would be confined to the townhouse with no visitors. She would take all her meals in the kitchen before he returned from work and then retire to her own room. She would help with the packing during the day as they'd be leaving town to move to a mansion called Sunnydale in Norristown, in the neighboring county.

Her head had reeled with confusion. She'd realized Norristown was at least a hard two-day walk, maybe more, from the farm. Robert's automobile, a luxury in the eyes of poor country folk, frightened her, yet gave her confidence that the distance would be manageable for her, although not for her mama. That is if she was allowed to use the vehicle. As her visible panic mounted, she'd witnessed a signal from Robert. Two housemaids grabbed her arms, holding her down as Eli approached with the shears. Walking to the door, Robert appeared satisfied.

"This will be a small taste of my displeasure if you become a nuisance." Turning smartly, he'd dismissively left the room. Eli had then scooped up a fistful of her long gleaming tresses and, with one hack, her hair had disappeared.

She'd become his captive, isolated from all she knew. Her days had consisted of packing and desperately staying out of Robert's sight. She'd realized the cropping of her hair was meant to demoralize her. He needn't have bothered. She'd been so traumatized, she appeared to be the walking dead, even spooking the household staff. Her nose had begun to heal without the benefit of medical care. As a result, the cant had fused permanently, throwing her pleasant features off balance, making her almost unrecognizable. It also left an unsightly bump on the bridge of her nose. The dull and lifeless hair left on her scalp had begun to show signs of small bald spots brought on by stress. Over time, they'd become permanent.

And the rapes had continued. Not frequently, for she realized Robert actually despised her. But once a week, he returned home at dawn, pleased with himself and more inebriated than usual. He'd routinely appeared at her bedside naked, his ugly purple erection stupid with desire. She'd dared not cry out for fear he'd punish her in some sick evil way. So she'd acquiesced, silently wanting to kill him.

Why, why, why me? What did I do wrong? Why has Mama not come to visit me? Did they turn her away at the door? Not knowing had driven her crazy. If only she could get a message to her mama, she and Mr. Woods would rescue her.

As much as a month had passed since her ill-fated wedding, and the household packing was finally completed. Netty had decided to bribe a young housemaid with one of the coins given to her by Mr. Woods. God bless the miracle that had made Robert neglect to search her belongings and appropriate her purse.

She'd painstakingly written a message to her mama in her childish block letters, hiding it in her apron pocket with the coin, planning to pass it along to her young accomplice, a kitchen wench she'd managed to discreetly befriend.

The hardwood floors squeaked. Spinning around, Netty had seen Robert standing in the doorway. *Oh Lord, did he see me hide the note?* His expression unreadable, she'd held her breath. Without preamble, he'd casually sat her in a chair and delivered the awful news. The sheriff had found her mama assaulted and murdered in their cabin. It appeared to have occurred several weeks ago. She need not plan a funeral; the body had already been interred. Netty had screamed, pitifully slumping to the floor.

Her cold silent tears brought Netty back to the present, sitting on the chilled floor of the lonely woods. Wiping away her useless teardrops, she carried on, not understanding the unrelenting compulsion. Her damaged feet continued to whimper their fruitless protest.

The cleft in the rocky hillside led her to the path that circled around a magnificent piece of granite, most likely deposited as glaciers moved across the continent during one of the many ice ages. The rock, a beacon to any child, had seduced her as well. It had become her private sanctuary. The place she ran to for dreaming, praying and saying goodbye to her creatures when her efforts to help their sufferings had failed.

Every creature she'd lost withered her young heart and caused her to rail at God for his indifference to the suffering of the innocent. In particular, her worst moments with God came after receiving a maimed creature, often dropped on her family's doorstop by a sympathetic neighbor, clearly intentionally harmed by someone. She knew instinctively that every creature was entitled to one thing: life. To steal that through abuse or indifference argued a crime against God. At her rock, she could cry or rail at God in private. As long as she was respectful to Him, she could exercise her frustration, vent, then return home to her makeshift hospital, ready to soldier on.

Sudden chattering from above drew her gaze. Two squirrels argued, probably over territory judging by the signals of their furious tail thumping. Brightening, she grasped the first handhold to climb the rock just as she'd done before her marriage. She gingerly pulled herself up, her eyes skimming over a pile of loose rocks at the base of the granite where it leaned into the hillside, something of a cairn that she didn't recall having seen before. Further on, she spied a fat rattlesnake sunning itself and coiled around the base of a young maple tree, frighteningly close to the pathway she would have to traverse on her way back out of the woods. She remembered the knoll was not called Snake Hill for nothing.

Reaching the top, she spotted the concave depression she'd used as a throne as a child. The seat was cold and sharp against her twenty-three-year-old rump. Suddenly, Netty saw another flash of rainbow color in the periphery of her vision, similar to the one that had visited her at the cabin. Was she coming down with something? Maybe a brain malady? She couldn't afford to get sick now, just as she was starting her new life. Memory returned to her last days at the mansion.

A truce of sorts had developed between her and Robert. Thankfully, he no longer demanded her attentions in the bedroom. They still lived in their Renaissance Revival mansion in Norristown, and occasionally she'd wandered the mansion at night while Robert was out late with his business partners. She'd loved admiring the high ceilings and beautiful carvings of their home, secretly investigating every nook and cranny.

She was forbidden to enter her husband's stunning library. The room was thirty eight by twenty five feet, and every inch of the dark oak walls was carved with intricate designs. The massive fireplace was dressed in an emerald-green marble surround with an amazing carved mantle that stretched all the way to the twelve-foot ceiling and which showcased Robert's valuable collection of antique American gold coins. She'd often spied him in the library, slobbering over them as if they were his children. The collection frequently impressed guests who'd stopped by to request favors or seek his advice.

She'd sat at her husband's extraordinary partners desk, the top made of the richest burled walnut. A partners lamp made by the talented Louis Comfort Tiffany rested comfortably where it could reflect the warmth of the fireplace. She'd pulled on the chain, casting light over the hand-carved body of the desk.

It was while admiring the intricate dark walnut carvings that she'd innocently discovered her husband's dark secrets. Accidently pressing a small carved bump that was part of the design on the inside wall of the cubby for her husband's legs, she'd discovered a secret panel. Upon excited investigation, she'd found the source of his unexplained wealth. It was certainly not family money as everyone had assumed. For inside the secret panel she'd also uncovered a shelf holding a copy of Robert's father's will.

Robert stood to inherit nothing. Except for the family townhouse, deeded to his five elder sisters, there was little of the Doyle fortune left. Expensive wedding dowries and even more expensive weddings had severely drained his father. Such was the cost of attracting suitably wealthy husbands. His sisters were set.

Netty had also uncovered receipts from the town clerk that showed Robert paid the taxes and upkeep of the family townhome, which had come as quite a surprise. *Hmm,* she thought, *Robert is not known to be generous.*

Upon further investigation, she'd found receipts for large sums of money to several town fathers and realized that he wielded much power and influence in their city. He ruled the county courthouse and was bowed and scraped to accordingly. Things started to add up, yet it made the question of why he'd married her even more mysterious. And what about the source of all of his money? Her suspicions had flamed wildly.

And there it had been, pushed to the very back of the secret drawer: a ledger, dog-eared and covered with spills, but legible. The ledger had contained payroll records, listing most of the names of his so-called friends and business partners. Taking in the columns of numbers along with dates and times, it had become clear. They were his employees. Last but not least had been a detailed account of shipping intake and disbursements. Glancing at the materials listed, any fool could have seen that her husband was a gin- and rum-runner. Law enforcement clearly rested in his back pocket. The late night partying at the carriage house now took on a new light. It also explained the presence of the thuggish strangers who'd seemed ever-present back there during the day.

Would it be possible to use this information to obtain her release? She'd often thought of murdering her husband to end her imprisonment, but knew she couldn't face her Lord if she took a life.

As she shuffled the papers and ledger back to their hiding place, her hands had dislodged an envelope she'd previously overlooked. Glancing at it quickly, she saw it was the last will and testament of James Woods; *her* Mr. Woods.

It had taken her many years to begin to heal from the death of her mother, and just as long to bury her hurt and disappointment over Mr. Woods' abandonment. Perhaps he'd thought that now she was married, her days occupied her to the exclusion of old friends. She'd failed time and time again to convince Robert to let her visit him. Finally, Robert confessed to her that Mr. Woods had passed away shortly after her mother's death. It was presumed to have been a heart attack, as he'd been found in an alley not far from his home. He added the rumor that the family had inherited a sizeable fortune.

Netty had run her fingers tenderly over Mr. Woods' name, wondering why his will was in Robert's possession.

Out of curiosity, Netty had opened the contents of the envelope. Most of the text seemed to have been written in a legalese and jargon unfamiliar to her. She'd recognized the names of members of Mr. Woods' family and could see he'd taken care of them.

Suddenly, she recognized her own name on the last page: Jeannette Elizabeth Woods Smith. *Woods? What is that all about? Quite an odd mistake.* Tears had dropped softly to her lap as she realized Mr. Woods had not forgotten her at all. Reading on, she learned that he'd bequeathed to her all the two thousand acres surrounding the cabin her family had lived in.

She'd been incredulous. *Why was I not told? When did this happen?* Netty looked for a date on the will. On the signature line, she read that Mr. Woods had signed it about five years before her marriage. And underneath his signature was her husband's name as attorney of record. The stunning truth: *he'd always known.*

Feeling a lump on her lap, she realized she'd overlooked more papers. Smoothing them out on the desk, a tiny map of the farm and their cabin unfolded. It had been attached to a message asking her husband to draw up the final contract for the transfer of Lots 1 thru 300, blocks 14 thru 46 to the O'Reilly Development Corp. *He is selling part of the farm: my farm?*

Netty considered the implications. Mr. Woods' family must have wondered about the strange bequest. They must have been aware of it. If the will legally conveyed title to the property, she'd been the legal owner for many years. Her thoughts and emotions had turned upside down with confusion while her sneaking anger had grown. She couldn't understand her husband's motives for hiding her inheritance. It left her only one choice. She must challenge him and wrench the truth from him.

Dare she hope that this might be the vehicle for her escape from her insufferable existence? She'd thought it might be, but she must take pains to be careful. Breathing deeply, she'd tried to calm down. She desperately needed to think straight.

Pocketing the evidence, she'd risen to her feet. Unnerved at the sound of the front door opening, she'd scampered out of the room and up the stairs to her bedroom. Frantically, she'd searched for the wedding purse she'd hidden away years ago. Yes, her silver coins were still there. She'd looked wildly around her small bedroom. Clothes; she needed suitable attire. She must be ready to run if things went wrong. Her nightclothes would not be seemly.

"*Netty.*" She'd heard her husband bellow loud enough to wake the dead, certainly the household staff. He'd sounded drunk as usual and more angry than normal. With no time to change, she'd scooped up a heavy woolen shawl, slipping her purse and the papers securely into a deep pocket.

Quickly, she'd descended to the foyer stairs where her husband waited. He'd stood at the entrance to the library, shaking with rage, his face purple and ready to explode. In his hands, he'd held papers. Her heart had fluttered painfully.

In her haste, she'd neglected to replace them in the secret drawer. Her courage had deserted her. This wasn't how she'd intended to pry information from him. She'd cowered at the thought of her lost advantage. Springing forward, Robert had painfully caught her wrist, dragging her into the room.

"Do you have any explanation as to why my private papers have been rifled through?"

Netty had ignored the question. Mustering a shaky voice, she'd confronted him. "I should like an explanation for this, Robert."

He'd appeared stunned to find the tiny map in her hand. She'd watched as the realization of her knowledge dawned across his face. Without any warning, he'd balled his hand into a fist, punching her hard in the stomach.

"I told you never to question me," he'd whispered, the venom in his voice dripping poison. Dragging her to a chair, she'd doubled over, unable to breathe. Robert screamed for Eli. It hadn't taken him long to appear, his leering grin a sign he'd hoped for some excitement. Looking wildly from Robert to Netty, he'd waited for a command. With a nod from Robert, Eli had put his meaty paws on her, holding her down with his well-muscled brown arms, his reeking breath bathing her neck while Robert paced.

This will not be good, Netty had thought as she'd tried to sit up. She'd been able to hear Robert muttering angrily under his breath. His words had grown louder as he'd increased his cursing. Her ears had perked up when she'd heard her mother's name; something about her mother being difficult.

Shapely . . . just get rid of her, but she tempted me . . . the tramp . . . firm thighs . . . spread her legs for James Woods when they were kids. Choking the life out of her . . . Satisfaction . . . brat to meet a similar fate.

Unthinking, Netty had cried out in shock. "You killed Mama? Why? Why?"

Robert's eyes had zeroed in on Netty. She'd cringed in her chair, Eli still holding her down. As Robert had moved to grab her, the front doorbell had rung. Robert froze, his hand raised to strike. He'd ordered Eli to answer the door.

They'd listened as Eli explained that Robert was indisposed. The men at the door insisted they see him as his presence was needed at the carriage house. To make matters worse for Robert, the chief of police had accompanied them, a little matter of his cut. Clearly, it would take Robert's intervention to make them go away, so he'd prepared to step into the foyer.

Hissing venomously to Netty as he'd left, he'd flayed her with his glinting eyes. *"Don't you dare move."*

Netty had sprung to her feet as soon as his back had been turned. She knew Robert's plan for her. Now she must run, even as she'd seethed with anger and shock over the night's revelations.

Glancing toward the fireplace, her eyes had caught the reflected glow of Robert's prized gold coins. Without thinking, she'd grabbed one, thrusting it into her undergarments, then dashed out the French door to the terrace.

From there she'd begun her long journey to Sussex County. Hiding in barns at night and staying to the wooded edge of the roads by day, she'd resolutely limped her way, stumbling over rocks and ruts, ignoring the protests of her tender bleeding feet.

Netty's thoughts were suddenly yanked back to the present. *Did I doze off?* She realized she'd dawdled away hours of valuable time with her reminiscing. The late afternoon air was cool and she knew it was time to get back to the cabin to light the evening's fire.

The small object still hidden under her bodice dug into her chest. She reached in to adjust it, first drawing it out to admire, the coin glinting in the late afternoon light. Yes, it was the coin she'd purloined from her husband's collection.

She hesitated to use it for cabin repairs, as it would draw too much attention. She suspected her husband might not come after her. After all, she legally owned the cabin now. But she'd no intention of giving him another excuse. She didn't want to be accused of robbery. People had a dim view of stealing in these parts, it was a serious crime.

Netty finally realized that Robert had only married her for the land. And it was now clear to her that her real father had been Mr. Woods. It explained so much. She loved her papa dearly, but she also loved Mr. Woods. She felt lucky to have had two good men in her life. Pulling up her bodice to replace the coin, it inexplicably slipped from her stiff, chilled fingers. *Lord!* She watched as it bounced off the rock and over the edge. She scrambled up to hear it ping on the rocks below. Leaning over, she saw it bounce all the way to the cairn of stones she'd noticed on her ascent up the path. It glinted in the sun, mocking her. There was no choice but to climb down and retrieve it. Rolling up the legs on her torn and faded trousers, she slipped down from the granite rock.

As Netty approached the cairn, she saw it was much larger than she'd first thought. She reached to pick up the coin, her fingers dislodging a stone, sending the coin deeper into the mound. Ugh, the prospect of digging the coin out lacked appeal. She wanted to go home to the cabin. Grumbling, she lowered herself to the ground, pushing stones out of her way. Progress was slow, her feet hurt and she quickly tired. The light dimmed as her digging created a large hole in the side of the hill. *Where's the darn coin?* Netty decided she'd come back tomorrow when she'd be stronger. This had proved to be a bigger job than she'd expected. Rising to her feet, she brushed off her apron. In the periphery of her vision she saw a flash of colored light. An aura. *Again?* Not knowing what to make of it, she shrugged to herself and prepared for the trek back to the cabin.

Chapter 2

The Oolahan tried to shake off its sleepy weariness. Its tiny limbs, withered and leather-like, coiled protectively around its cooling body. Its small round head, perched upon its swiveled neck, was devoid of the fur that normally protected its face. Its perfectly round eyes, with their abundant lashes missing, were shut tight. It could feel that the fluid in its body was still low, making its eyes dry and cracked, its vision useless. Its long dense tail thumped weakly, unable to expel its healing light waves, although it could not project them on to itself, anyway.

Scattered around the great cavern were the large black fragments of its transport. It had no idea how long it had been in the cavern. It felt an urgency to begin the implementation of its mission, but unfortunately the details of the purpose eluded it. Sensing its presence, the creature thought perhaps the Womb could help. Why hadn't it given him instructions? It needed help to recover and remember the mission.

Taking matters into its own hands, it decided to summon help. It sensed that the life force to which it called might be close. It didn't worry, as it knew the life force would find its way eventually.

The creature ruminated, remembering its Brothers and Sisters back home. Many of the Oolahan were preparing for breeding. Breeding, a critical necessity for the Womb, meant death for the Oolahan. Once upon a time, the Oolahan had enjoyed immortality. They became Elders, learning the skills of the Womb, instead of being minions. Creativity exploded. So much could be done for life with so many solar systems to work with.

Disaster occurred when the Elders had decided to use their own genetic material to experiment with. Their experiment introduced one of the most destructive elements ever seen on a fertile planet.

Unfortunately, the planet happened to be a long time favorite of the Womb.

As a result, the Womb had punished the Oolahan, denying them the privilege of immortality. A protein was introduced into their system, nullifying the hormones and enzymes that enabled their forever life. And they were forbidden to ever heal the results of their ill-fated experiment. Through the act of healing, it was discovered that the Oolahan could accidently pass to the life form the very protein that unlocked the introduced enzymes which triggered immortality.

The Womb agreed not to destroy the life form, only to monitor them until it became intolerable. The forbidden life form was not the only life that grew out of control. When a species on any world overwhelmed another to the point of extinction, or imbalance, the Womb would intervene.

Often, it meant the elimination of the offending species, and then the Womb would rain destruction, allowing new life to take its turn at evolution.

The Oolahan didn't need to breed, as their numbers were enough to satisfy the Womb. But once they had been stripped of immortality, they began to die. Their only recourse was to breed their own replacements. Since they had originally been created by the Womb to act as its minions, the only way to breed was by incubating a cell from the host; a simple matter. The new cell was then implanted inside the dying Oolahan, taking nourishment from the host until it was ready to emerge, bringing about the eventual death of the host Oolahan.

Each Oolahan prepared a life cell then expertly implanted themselves: their talent was creating life. It was an intensely personal matter. After implantation was deemed successful and the cell was dividing well, the breeding was announced. Upon Emergence, the Oolahan Brothers and Sisters preserved the afterbirth with its valuable cells, took charge of the new naive Oolahan and monitored the disposition of the deceased, who would expire within a very short time.

This Oolahan had missed the opportunity to report its Breeding before it was chosen for the mission. Easily overlooked in the excitement of its preparations, the breeding had remained unreported. Signs of life inside the minion became apparent after it had started its journey to this world. But it alone had been aware of its condition. Had its condition been known, it would have been rejected for the flight.

It knew the Emergence had occurred sometime after landing. Evidence of dried and useless afterbirth abounded. Had it been conscious during the Emergence, the healing waves of the afterbirth might have prolonged its life. If the Emergence had occurred back home, it would have been surrounded by Brothers and Sisters, experts in the science of rechanneling. The rechanneling of waves from the afterbirth had the ability to prolong life for a short time, long enough to make preparations to salvage its valuable cells. It should have expired by now. For some strange reason, it still lived, although just barely. Either way, the mission had been doomed from the start. The creature wondered how long it had to live as it continued to sort out the confusion of its circumstances.

Apparently, hibernation and the birth had changed its body chemistry, altered it in some fashion upon successful landing and burrowing. Or had it been caused during the entry into this different atmosphere? Was it because of the new Oolahan's Emergence? Did the fact that Emergence had happened on this new planet somehow interfere with the chemical compounds in its system?

Not being genetically programmed for maternal or paternal feelings, it didn't show concern about the whereabouts of its offspring. But it did worry about its mission. Maybe in time it could sort things out, but right now it needed to concentrate on attracting the life force to it. It needed its sustenance.

It was not within the fabric of its species to hurt living creatures. Its species revered all life. For an eternity, their sole purpose had been to study and enhance life. The Elders had been fiercely ambitious. The creature suspected its mission had something to do with the changes in its species' priorities since the life-altering mistake of the Elders. Their attention had turned from their business in the stars to their own survival. At the moment, the creature had no idea how the details of its mission could be recovered. So it decided to meet one necessity at a time.

The creature tried to lift its confused head, bringing on a sharp pain accompanied by dizziness. It had somehow been damaged. It felt its useless wings crumpled and cramped under its tiny body. It tried desperately to remember something about the life forms of this planet. Unable to focus, it wondered if it was due to the unexpected presence of its offspring, the atmosphere of the planet or complications during the Emergence. *Oh, did I already have that thought?*

As the creature drew in the life form, it planned to take what was needed and leave the life form essentially unchanged for now. The current in its veins quickened as its crystal-like antlers picked up the distant sounds. The sounds were very faint, the entrance to its shelter being so far away and at a different elevation. Soon the next chapter of its mission would start, but sadly, it had little hope for success, as its death, due to the Emergence, was probably not far off.

Netty labored long and hard to remove stones and larger rocks from what appeared to be the entrance to a tunnel. She felt dog tired. How or why she continued was beyond her comprehension. The sun had set hours ago and the cold numbed her fingers. *Who in the world dug a tunnel way out here and why should I care?* Her poor feet screamed, her sores begging for a good soaking. Netty found she could now stand in the mouth in the tunnel.

Straightening up and standing tall, she realized she could actually see inside what should have been a pitch-black interior. Reaching out, she touched one of the walls, feeling its hard, compressed and slightly burnt texture. She quickly withdrew her hand as the wall felt suddenly squishy and wet. Examining her hand, she found it bone dry.

Quickly moving away from the strange wall, she took tiny steps into the tunnel. As she shuffled along, she noticed the absence of debris on the floor. *Odd,* she thought. *And why is it that I have no trouble seeing in the dark?* Actually, it no longer appeared to be night. It seemed to be more like daylight. *What is this place?*

She trudged on, noticing tunnels branching off the main artery into many other directions. A quick peek astonished her with the breadth and the height of the other branches. She must be careful or she'd get lost.

She then found herself crossing a huge cathedral of a cavern. Time passed as she continued on, sticking to the main artery. From time to time, she rubbed her hand along a normal-looking wall. The harder she pressed it, the deeper her hand disappeared. Yet each time her hand remained dry when withdrawn. She eventually noticed a distinct change of grade, signaling her descent. Her shivering ceased as the cave chased away her chill.

Netty suddenly stopped her trek. She turned to the right, noticing a small opening to what appeared to be a chamber. Puzzled about an irresistible compulsion which unexpectedly gripped her, she paused, then entered the chamber.

Clearing the little opening, she gasped at the sight of what appeared to be a dead infant lying on a rock ledge. As she approached the child, she realized her first impression had been wrong. It was not a child at all, she could clearly make out a tail. She edged closer, her heart going out to the poor creature, which had probably found an opening to the cavern and crawled inside to die, safely away from the forest predators. *But what such creature is this?* The tiny shriveled body was unrecognizable. It was obviously female, as she didn't see any signs of genitalia. She strangely saw no overt signs of decay. Cradling the creature's head in her hands, she prayed over it, asking God to accept another of his children into his arms.

As Netty's eyes were clenched in prayer, she failed to notice the creature's tail rising. She tenderly cradled the creature's head, feeling sudden warmth. Opening her eyes, she saw the little creature's limbs had unfurled and taken on a rosy golden hue, although the texture still looked like that of dissected leather.

Suddenly, she spotted the tail hanging in the air. The end was now shaped like a large bulb, extruding a thick fibrous membrane. She felt a wave of pressure and detected a stinky aroma. *Good heavens, the creature is alive.* Startled, but not yet frightened, she dropped the creature back on the rock ledge, stepping back. As she watched, the creature slowly opened its eyes. They then shut, just as slowly, as if in great pain. A weak mewing sound emanated from its body, yet its mouth failed to move.

Netty felt suddenly weak and fell down flat on her generous bottom, her skin tingling. The creature's eyes opened again and watched her. It didn't move. *Perhaps it cannot*, she thought. *Maybe I should take it home.* She could nurse it back to health. They stared at each other for several minutes; the creature on the ledge, Netty on the chamber floor. She wondered how long she'd been inside the cavern. She should be getting home to bed, but realized she no longer felt bone tired. Standing up, she discovered her feet no longer hurt, either. She dismissed her good fortune, grateful she'd now have the strength to walk back through the cavern and home with the tiny creature in her arms.

Brushing herself off, she approached gingerly, trying not to frighten the creature. Carefully, she slid her hands under its sunken belly, giving extra support to its head. It mewed again. Looking into its expressionless face, it blinked then stared at her, but offered no protest. *Easy* she thought, *I do not want it to bite me, although it looks like it surely does not have the strength.* She placed the creature up over her shoulder, as you would an infant, and gently rubbed its back to reassure it.

"There, there, little girl, Netty will take care of you." Slipping off her apron, she placed it around the little creature's pitiful shoulders and started her trek out of the cavern and back home.

The Oolahan had felt the emotions of the life source as it headed toward The Hive. It could feel the life source was benevolent but in pain. That always made things more difficult. It knew pain made other creatures unpredictable and dangerous. It couldn't have that.

A noise outside its chamber had announced the arrival. The life source stepped into sight. It was a female, a Sister, a mature one. Could that make a difference? She was staring, seemingly transfixed. *That is good, a little closer,* it prayed. *And yes.* The Sister placed her hands on the Oolahan, allowing it to suck in the life-giving energy that would nourish it back to health. *How did she know?* How wonderfully easy. Since its tail now had enough energy to expel, it let loose on the Sister in a gesture of gratitude, completely forgetting it was forbidden by The Womb.

It could sense great worry from the Sister. *Why is that? Can she not see?* The Oolahan stared at her as it tried to understand her actions. The Sister stared back. It felt the Sister picking it up. It panicked, mewing a complaint, then relaxed as the Sister rubbed its back.

Things are clearly out of control, the Oolahan thought as it helplessly felt the Sister place a cloth over its body. It remained motionless as the Sister walked out of the cavern with the Oolahan over her shoulder.

Chapter 3

Netty struggled with the unwieldy broken door of the cabin, juggling the creature as she fought with the warped boards that were her protection from the elements. The creature had made no further sound as she trudged with her burden from the woods, her wayward gold coin having been returned to its hiding place under her bodice.

She moved directly to her old straw mat by the fireplace. Fresh straw and a good sweep and dusting had made the room serviceable. Much of her mama's possessions had been ransacked or stolen. Having purchased a used rocker and some pots, she knew a warm fire and something in their stomachs was all they needed for now.

She set the creature gently on the straw mat and got busy making a fire. Soon, the cabin filled with the sounds of crackling wood and warm air that aggressively pushed away the evening chill.

Netty finally had time to sit in her split-oak rocker as her dinner pot simmered over the fire. She studied the creature as it appeared to study her, its expressive eyes now appearing bright and swirly with golden hues. *How odd, yet beautiful.* The little thing had looked dead, but she'd clearly been mistaken. She reminded herself what she knew from hard experience: whatever injury or illness gripped the odd creature could still bring about its death.

Netty decided she must give the poor thing an exam. She approached it carefully, although she no longer feared it would bite. She saw its limbs appeared shrunken and withered with a sort of attachment at the end of what appeared to be its legs. The attachment looked like a foot of sort, but it wobbled when she moved it. *Is it broken?*

The creature didn't appear to feel any pain when she wiggled it. She examined its head, noticing that it wiggled like the foot. She gently turned its body to the side to examine underneath. As she did so, she noticed the creature's head turning to follow. And turn and turn. *That cannot be. It is a physical impossibility.*

Looking closer, she found the creature simply had a different type of bone structure, allowing its head to rotate around the body, as its feet probably could too. On the creature's back, she found herself amazed by a crumpled structure that almost appeared to be tiny leathery wings; *the poor thing.* She wondered what unfortunate fate had come knocking at the creature's door. She picked up the creature's lovely tail. Since they'd left the woods, a subtle sheen had colored its crinkled leathery skin, fine golden hairs sprouting. Its abdomen was now round and gold, firm to the touch. The striking similarity between its hands and those of the great apes from the dark continent of Africa entranced her.

The differences jumped out at her. She wanted to touch the very fragile and elongated fingers with itty, bitty fingernails just like hers. Turning them over she could make out tiny dark swirls that actually looked like a device for suction. *Interesting . . .*

Taking the creature's head in her hands, she stroked what looked like golden fuzz on its head, stopping at the point where two glittery antlers emerged from the rear of its head, growing forward and twining together like a crown. They almost looked like they were made of glass. *How can that be?*

The creature suddenly smiled at her, and she felt her bruised and withered heart miss a beat. Continuing the exam, she decided it surely looked like an odd and improbable creature. *Well, I am an odd creature myself, am I not?*

But it must have a name. In the back of Netty's mind, she was mulling over the idea of keeping the creature. It smiled again which transformed Netty's loneliness for a brief moment. She didn't know where it came from or what it was, but she already loved it.

That settled the matter. She felt desperately lonely and this poor creature needed her. It was probably a baby. She needed a baby. So it was settled. She would call it Baby. In the back of her head she heard the echo, "Bay-bee," a whisper of golden colors, like an aura. Netty shook her head, cursing her sleepiness.

She hurriedly spooned up some vegetable broth from her cooking kettle over the fire, swallowing quickly. She placed a bowl of water at the side of the straw mat for Baby and took herself off to bed after banking the fire and making sure the door to the cabin was firmly shut. Tomorrow would bring plenty of chores to catch up on.

Baby lay quietly on the straw mat. He found himself quite comfortable. The tall Sister's behavior had been non-threatening. He wondered what he was to do with the bowl she'd left next to the mat. Was it for him? He sat up, spilling the liquid on the floor. He realized how unsteady he still was. Ignoring the spilled liquid, he put the bowl on his head, hooking it over his crown of antlers.

He decided to stay and observe the Sister and see where this relationship would go. He'd no idea as to his offspring's whereabouts. The urgency of his mission slowly began to fade. Perhaps if he'd been a Sister, his recovery since landing would have been different. But he was here now and knew he needed the tall Sister's hand on him again until he found a new energy source. As he recovered, he would hear her more fully in his mind. Fleetingly, he wondered how much longer he would live until his expiration.

Looking around the small room, he wondered where Sister had disappeared to. Spotting the door to Netty's bedroom, he hopped up from the straw mat and worked at the door handle with his long thin fingers. His feet made soft plunks as he wobbled his way over to the jumbled platform she rested upon. Placing one foot on the bed frame, he twisted his entire body to a perpendicular level as his hands gripped the covers, placing his other foot higher on the frame until he swiveled to the top of the bed. Carefully burrowing under the blanket into the curve of Netty's belly, he promptly went to sleep.

Netty woke, feeling the best she had since, well, since she'd been a young girl, working on the farm with her mama and papa. The memory warmed her and she stretched heartily.

"Oh." Shocked to feel something hard and cold in bed with her, she reached under her covers, pulling out the bowl she'd left at

Baby's bedside. Ripping off the covers, she discovered Baby curled up and looking up at her wide-eyed. Baby's eyelashes were now quite pronounced with thick, shimmering golden hairs. Golden fur sprouted all over her head tapering to uniform fuzz, covering her entire body. Her leathery extremities were now soft and supple having filled out. Even her concave abdomen had plumped up, giving her a little tummy. As Netty watched, Baby solemnly picked up the bowl and placed it back on her head atop her crown of antlers. Then Baby smiled. Netty sat stunned. Charmed and enchanted, she gathered Baby into her arms as tears rolled down her cheeks. Baby's long fingers traced the path of a tear, the bowl falling off her head. A flash of rainbow light and a pressure in her head shattered the moment. The pressure lessened, leaving a golden aura and a whispered word, seemingly from inside her head.

"Sister?"

Netty, confused, whipped her head around, finally resting her eyes on Baby. *It cannot be. Am I going mad?*

They sat, just staring at one another. Netty finally reached out to stroke Baby again, with wonder and amazement. She sensed the pressure in her mind recede, leaving a softer presence. Timidly, she tried to relax her mind. As Baby continued to stare intently, she felt a whisper.

"I am Brother."

Brother? Baby is a little boy?

"Yes, my Sister."

Is the presence reading my thoughts? The aura faded. Netty's mind felt empty as she searched its corners, frantic to find the golden aura. *Nothing.* Baby just stared, his golden rainbow eyes unblinking.

Well, Netty thought, *this is a puzzle. Has my debilitated condition allowed my mind to play tricks on me?* Warily, she decided to be patient, the answers would come. At least she realized she didn't need to worry about healing Baby. He seemed to have done just fine on his own.

Time to put the kettle on the fire, she thought, leaving Baby on her bed and wondering if she'd imagined the words in her head. She wrapped her robe tightly around her as the morning chill depressed her with the memory of the overwhelming work she still faced.

The cabin warmed as her breakfast kettle simmered. She wondered what Baby might need to eat. Ruefully, she realized she was ill equipped to take care of this magnificent creature, so different from all the other woodland creatures she'd ever tended. *How did I miss this one?* she wondered. Perhaps he was just rare. *Oh well, he belongs with me now, unless he decides to return to the woods.* Netty dismissed the discovery of the giant cavern as none of her business.

She returned to the bedroom to wash and change into her work clothes. Glancing toward the bed, she saw that Baby had moved to her pillow, perching on it with his golden legs crossed, just like a little man. *Oh, maybe Baby is not an infant.* She went to him, picking him up to kiss his face. He made a chuffing sound, but sent no more whispers.

With a last kiss and cuddle, Netty set Baby back on the bed. She moved to a simple cupboard in the corner of the room to remove another pair of her papa's overalls which had been overlooked by the looters. Slipping off her nightgown, she observed a slightly trimmer waist than she was used to seeing. Not surprised, she considered her flight from her husband's clutches, her hard work and the meager meals she now afforded herself. Moving over to her washstand, she dipped her cloth into water warmed from the fire. She loved the feeling of the cloth suffusing the water's warmth into her skin. As she dawdled at the washstand, she felt thrown by the unfamiliar feeling of her nose through the washcloth. Something felt wrong; different.

Dropping the cloth from her hands, she peered into the mirror over the wash bowl, speechless. Her nose looked as straight as it had been on the day of her birth, the bump nonexistent. It was the old Netty looking back at her, albeit older. Suddenly, remembering her previous night's activities, she looked down at her feet. They were devoid of any scabs or sores, not to mention the pain that had disappeared last night. She whirled to her bed and stared at Baby. *Can it be?* She sat down, picking up Baby's tail, remembering the pressure in the chamber and the strange smell. She sniffed Baby's tail fur, not seeing the strange membrane from last night, but clearly smelling a faint trace of sulfur.

Stunned, Netty backed away from Baby, her thoughts in a whirl. Obviously elated over the changes in her appearance and overwhelmed with the happiness Baby's presence portended, these miracles defied logic. *Wait, that's it.* They were just miracles, not a sign of the devil as she'd begun to fear. Miracles were sent by God. She ran to Baby and stared into his amazing eyes; whirling colors glimmering at her. She felt a tentative touch in her mind.

"God?" Baby whispered.

"Yes." Netty felt relief course through her body. "God, our Father."

"Father." The aura sent the whisper into her mind.

"Yes, our Father protects us all, we are all his children," she said.

"Offspring?" Baby whispered.

"Yes, yes, Baby, we are all one," cried Netty.

"Yes, the Womb," her mind whispered, golden aura dancing. "Womb is father. Father, Brother, Sister." Baby smiled. And Netty smiled. Somehow, they'd made a breakthrough. She didn't know what 'the Womb' meant, but did it really matter? She knew everything would be just fine.

As Netty gathered her tools for her day's work, she ladled out a portion of breakfast porridge for Baby. Baby ignored it, spending his time following closely at her heels and inspecting everything she touched. Netty stepped out the door on to her stoop. The air contained a vague coolness, but the bright sun and translucent blue sky would soon warm her up. Planning to head to her family's old orchard to survey what might be salvaged, she noticed Baby had lain down on the stoop, arms outstretched. She called out to him with no response. Bending over to shake him, she felt rigidity. She bent over, intending to return him to her bed, when she felt the golden aura in her mind.

"Sister, I am eating."

Netty looked closer. She could actually see dust motes dancing in what looked like rays being absorbed into Baby's leathery extremities.

"Hungry, Sister. My eating is slow. Go. I will find you."

Netty felt a sense of wellbeing flood her mind. So, leaving Baby, she made her way to the orchard. Work couldn't stop just because she couldn't understand what Baby thought he was eating.

Netty made her way down the road and over the slight rise to take a look at the orchard. Her family had harvested many apples, pears and her favorite black walnuts for years. She had vivid memories of removing the yellow-green husk of the walnut with its icky messy black underside, and cracking the shell to get to the fresh tart-sweet meat. Her mama used the meat in her baking, stews and breads, claiming the nut was a wonderful substitute for costly trips to Mr. Simpson's butcher's shop in town.

Mr. Simpson was a scary man. He never smiled unless he was wielding his big knives on the carcass of a poor creature. His wife appeared to be terrified of him. At any rate, Netty wanted to stay away from town as much as possible. The walnut grove would be a great help to her diet.

Netty knew Sussex County had experienced blight a few years back. It hadn't spread to Norris County so she was unaware of the extent of the devastation. Hopefully, her orchard had been spared. As she topped the hill, her hopes sank. As far as she could see, her trees were nude, with only a few lonely leaves clinging hopelessly to the diseased branches. Worse yet, the trees were deformed and displayed huge hardened growths spilling from the trunks, obviously a symptom of the blight. She realized the canning supplies she'd purchased on her last walk to town wouldn't be filled with the fruits and jams she'd need to help get her through the winter as she'd planned.

Discouraged, she turned and started back to the cabin, planning to spend the rest of the day turning over soil in another field. She knew large supplies of seeds remained buried in caskets, hidden in the ground inside her former animal hospital. She hoped to plant enough to sell the surplus to travelers on the road into town.

Glancing up, she saw Baby heading toward her from the bottom of the hill, his little feet clumping and wobbling at the same time. She sat and waited for him to reach her. She saw the rainbow flash in her mind's eye, and heard the whisper.

"Sister sad?"

Gathering Baby into her lap, she buried her face in his fur. The little rascal actually looked plump. As he smiled at her with rainbow eyes glowing, she noticed he didn't have any teeth. Prying open his mouth she discovered he had no tongue. Removing her hands from his mouth, she wondered how he could eat or drink. Baby certainly puzzled her.

"Come along, Baby, we have much to do today." She stood, ready to head home. Looking down, she saw Baby still sitting with his mouth wide open. She gently reached down and, with her fingertips, she closed his mouth. Laughing, she thought about how happy and lighthearted he made her feel, even in the face of discouragement. As she walked back to the cabin, she turned to see if Baby followed. Yes, he shuffled behind, rotating his head on its swivel, allowing him to stare at the fading orchard as he followed Netty home.

After a quick lunch of cold porridge leftover from breakfast, Netty retired with Baby to the field she'd begun to till the day before. As she collected the larger of the fieldstones, piling them to the side of the field, Baby observed her intently.

"Food?" he probed in her mind.

"No, Baby, we are going to plant seed in the soil to *grow* our food." Progress was slow, but as she tilled the soil she could smell the rich organic loam. *Hard work never killed anyone,* she thought, energized by the idea of the independence her crops could provide her.

As the afternoon wore on, she made excellent progress. The part of the field she was working in was now clear of rock. She raked the smaller stones to the side, adding to her pile of rock which she planned to use as field boundary markers. She knew her papa and Mr. Woods never wasted anything on the farm. Everything had a purpose. Even the weeds from the field would be used in her giant compost pile. If this season's planting were successful, it would enable her to sell more at her stand. Her fervent hope was to purchase a horse to help her plow the field next season.

Netty found herself filled with new hope and plans for her success; an overwhelming change from yesterday. And she knew she had Baby to thank. She reached up to happily rub her nose, smiling at him as he lay rigidly stretched out under an oak tree. *Eating again*, she laughed to herself. She felt feather fingers stroke her mind, the golden aura infusing her.

"Yes, Sister."

Oops, I had better watch that, not much privacy with Baby.

Netty realized Baby had brought a big lift to her spirits. The fact that he spoke to her without using words was an unexplained phenomenon. Yet, for the first time in years, she dared to think that she wasn't alone. She knew she would go to bed tonight with anticipation for the new day instead of the normal dread.

Maybe tomorrow she could begin some planting. She'd like to get a jump on the season, then continue clearing the field. Calling to Baby, she picked up her tools and started home. It had been quite a day.

As Netty approached the door to the cabin, she dropped her tools, planning to open up the seed caskets and scope out her selections for the morning. Some of the beans would require soaking overnight before they could be planted.

Walking to the back field, she let herself into her makeshift hospital, now used strictly for storage. Taking a trowel, she went to the earthen floor under the single window where she knew her papa used to store the seed. Scraping off the top few inches of soil, she exposed the caskets. Even though they were really half caskets, they were still terribly heavy.

Lifting them out of their hole, she lined them up and popped the lids. They came off unusually easily. One sniff of the seeds told the story. Rot. She spilled a casket on to the floor. Most of the seeds were covered with a layer of mold. She was unable to tell how many of the seeds were still good, unwilling to waste precious energy and tilled space to plant bad seeds in the hope they might germinate.

Her exultant mood evaporated. She dispiritedly left the animal hospital, passing by Baby as she let herself into the cabin. Baby's neck swiveled toward the hospital. Realizing he'd remained outside, Netty returned to the door to call to him. The last thing she recalled before the pressure hit her was Baby's golden tail in the air.

Netty picked herself up from the floor, having landed on her bottom again. She detected the same odor she remembered from the cavern. Sulfur. *What just happened? Did it mean something?* Netty stood rooted to the spot, confusion immobilizing her as Baby strolled past her to the straw mat at the fireplace as if nothing had happened.

Well, she shrugged. *I guess that means it is time for dinner.* Putting on the dinner pot, she grabbed a potato from the bin. She wondered if Baby would eat something this time. Putting out a bowl of water for him, she completed dinner and served it on her rickety table. Baby shuffled to the table, again wearing the water bowl on his head. Netty dropped her spoon and laughed. Maybe someday Baby would tell her what it meant. She finished dinner, noticing Baby didn't touch his soup. Clearing the dishes, she dried her hands and headed to the outhouse to make her nightly ablutions.

As she opened the outhouse door, first looking for rattlesnakes, it occurred to her that she'd seen no signs that Baby had the same necessity. Assuming Baby was simply a woodland creature she'd never encountered before, she took herself off to bed. *Why worry over something that really does not matter?* she thought. She was beginning to love Baby even as he continued to mystify her. Her last thought that evening was how comforted she felt with Baby again pressed up against her as he slept curled under the covers by her tummy.

Netty and Baby woke the next morning to another beautiful day. Unfortunately, Netty's outlook for her planting was so low that she found climbing out of bed a miserable chore. She planned to sift through the seeds to see if she could find a few that might be salvageable. If she had to spend any of the last of her silver coins on new seed, she could have great difficulty stocking in the supplies she'd need to get the two of them through the winter.

As it was, she would lose her opportunity to get a jump on the planting. By the time she'd traveled back and forth to town and planted the new seed, she could lose a full week. She knew she couldn't take Baby to town with her and was unwilling to leave him alone just yet, afraid he might decide to return to the woods if she left him. She couldn't bear the thought.

Shrugging into her work clothes after breakfast, she grabbed a small basket from the kitchen to store the few seeds she hoped to salvage from the caskets. She noticed Baby was already stretched out on the stoop in what was becoming his customary eating position. *Whatever that means,* she thought. Arriving in front of her old animal hospital, she slid the sliding wood door completely back to let in as much sunlight as possible. As she stood in the small room, she didn't at first grasp what her eyes registered, not fully adjusted to the dimness. Slowly, awareness crept over her and she sank to her knees. Reaching out, she gingerly touched the little plants that lay all over the ground where yesterday she'd spilled moldy seeds. *This cannot be.* She quickly ran to the other caskets and found them chock full of little plants, all looking to burst out of their confinement and reach for the sun. Netty ran for the broken wheelbarrow she'd paid to have repaired. She hurriedly loaded it to the brim, worrying about their survival with no soil or water. No time to ponder on this new miracle, she quickly started down the road to her field, shouting to Baby as she passed him on the stoop.

By the time Baby made it to the field, she'd one beautiful row of seedlings in the ground and was digging holes for the second row. Distracted, she hardly noticed Baby, who approached the field, shining eyes focused intently on her as she planted. As she straightened up, wiping grime off her face, she watched as Baby made a hole with his fragile little fingers, plucked a plant from the wheelbarrow and buried it. Astonished and elated, Netty briefly wondered who had taught this to Baby.

Before long, Netty found herself running back to the hospital to refill the wheelbarrow and pick up lunch as Baby continued to do the planting. By late afternoon, Netty dripped with exhaustion. She glanced at Baby, now curled up inside the empty wheelbarrow and grinning at her with his amazing eyes doing their usual flashing. As tired as she felt, she still retained enough energy to scoop him into her arms and rub her face against his. Holding him on her hip like a mother would a child, she swung around to admire their work: row upon row of glowing greenery: corn, tomatoes, squash, beans, peppers, radishes, onions, watermelon, and honeydew. Even patches of strawberries and raspberries. *Hmm*, Netty thought, *the plants sure appear taller from where I stand.*

"Sister, eat," came the whispered aura in her mind.

"Yes, yes, yes." She laughed. "Soon, Baby. Now we must be patient while we wait for the plants to mature. We sure did a good job." Turning her back to the crops, she plunked Baby down into the wheelbarrow and started down the road.

Her thoughts were happy ones, full of a hopeful future. Now she felt they stood a chance. Funny how she automatically thought in terms of *they*. Yes, they could be a family, the two of them.

She took a deep breath, drawing in the sweet twilight air, reminiscence of apple blossoms. She stopped suddenly; *apple blossoms?* She turned her nose and sniffed, the smell deliciously overpowering.

Dropping the wheelbarrow, she sprinted up the hill where the road to the orchard branched off, struck dumb by her discovery.

Tall with straight clean trunks they stood, bursting with blossoms: apple, crab apple, pear and wild cherry, and her beloved black walnut grove. *This is impossible. What is going on here?* Her gaze thoughtfully fell on Baby as he followed her to the top of the hill. She stared back at the orchard, dumbfounded by the impossibility, yet acknowledging a slow dawning of outrageous gratitude and smug security creeping into her consciousness as she began to accept their assured future.

Suddenly, she sobered, her joy vanishing. She felt a chill and shivered. *Could this be magic or the devil's work after all?* Subdued, she gathered her wheelbarrow and made her way back to the cabin while her mind spun with confusion and possibilities.

Netty sat in her rocking chair, pressed up to the evening fire with Baby as he lay on his spot on the straw mat. It was time for her to make some decisions and put this issue to bed. She realized she was a simple woman, but she truly felt that all creatures, including people, were created by God. Without warning, a sleepy singsong whisper sang in her mind, a golden aura suffusing her mind's vision.

"God is Father, Father is Womb."

Netty reached over to Baby, shushing him. She needed a clear mind as she sorted out her feelings. She knew the country was young, much of it still not fully explored. There were many creatures that had probably only just been discovered and the knowledge of them not yet widely known; such as Baby.

Looking closely at Baby, she realized he didn't resemble, in whole or in part, anything she'd seen before. He could walk upright (*and perpendicular,* she thought wryly) and his hands were similar enough to hers that he could perform tasks; basically fairly normal, although his eyes were certainly difficult to explain. *What about my seeds and the miracle in the orchard?* God does give miracles, but the presence of Baby seemed more than a coincidence.

As an afterthought, she rubbed her nose. This morning, upon awakening, she'd noticed what appeared to be peach fuzz on her head, filling in her bald spots. What more good fortune could happen to her? Not suspicious by nature, her natural inclination was to accept what had clearly been sent by God. Should she take Baby back to the woods? What would that prove? Maybe Baby portended a good luck charm. *Her* good luck charm; yes, hers. Netty lay down next to Baby on the straw mat, scooping him into her arms. His warm little body shuddered, seemingly with relief. Netty's heart felt full and complete as she carried Baby to bed.

Netty and Baby's days passed with plenty of hard work. Netty ripped down a shed next to the barn, using the material to build her fruit stand on the road into town. Her crops were coming in gloriously. Her blossoms in the orchard produced huge lovely fruits, ripening splendidly in the sun. Her fruit trees evinced an unexpected growth spurt, adding the height and girth needed to support the huge luscious fruits they spawned. And her berry patches ripened for picking, a mere half handful all that was needed to fill a pie. It was an exciting time. Her berry pies, baked in her mama's bread oven were selling like crazy. She could not make them fast enough.

She constructed a special picnic basket for Baby to hide in while she spent time with customers at the fruit stand. Word of her pies and amazing fruit traveled to town. The owner of one of the popular local taverns took it upon himself to ride out in his shiny new automobile to see her. She was now his exclusive supplier of fresh fruit pies. And he wanted to be the first to see her vegetable crop come harvest time.

Netty was so busy, she hardly noticed that she'd slimmed down to a hard and strong figure. Easy to miss since she still wore the same clothes as when she'd met Baby. Unnoticed, her eyes took on a golden cast. Her hair grew long and lush, always pulled back and swept up in a ponytail, just like her mama's. Oddly, her hair seemed to be changing color as it grew in. It looked like spun gold. Hard-won pride left a pretty smile on her face. Her days got better and better.

Baby stretched quietly in his picnic basket. He gave up trying to remember the purpose of his mission. He casually wondered about the whereabouts of his offspring. Not that it mattered. His species was fully prepared to face life upon Emergence, as they were born with the memory of their eternal history.

His life with his new Sister passed quite pleasantly, those of his species weren't meant to be alone. He didn't understand many of her customs, but not much seemed to be required of him, so he fell into an easy routine. Shockingly, he began to accept the fact that, here on this planet, his physiology behaved differently. Luckily, it appeared he no longer ran the risk of expiration.

Occasionally, his mind turned back to the moment he'd met his new Sister. He felt a twinge of fear as he realized the life force he'd called to feed on had turned out to be a Sister; a grave mistake as it was forbidden to heal a human.

He should have waited before sending her his grateful healing. He wondered if he'd angered the Womb with his carelessness. Unfortunately, he'd not been able to stop himself when she'd touched him, and had automatically helped himself to her life force. That in itself was allowed. It was just the bad timing of the state of what Sister called *eating*, the unexpected changes to his molecular structure brought on by his penetration into this new atmosphere, and the shocking discovery that his tail had fully evolved.

Only Elders sported fully evolved tails. Only Elders could heal other organisms. The control over his tail nonexistent and the ability to discriminate temporarily arrested had led to her healing. He knew it was sinful to heal a Sister of this planet, so he kept careful eyes on her, watching for the signs. So far, her changes didn't frighten him. If she began to develop signs of an Elder, he knew the Womb might decide to take action. He had no idea what the Womb might do to punish him. After all, it was well known throughout most universes that the Womb resented the humans because of the defiance their creation represented.

Addressing his attention to his tail again, he felt the weight of the new membrane, all doubt removed. It was fully mature and functioning. He'd tested it on the Sister's trees that had been dying, and on the tiny buttons she called seeds. Some were already dead. No help for them. But the rest were easy to correct. A gift, he did it happily for Sister; she'd seemed so distraught over the dead ones. He recognized they involved something to do with her eating. He knew how important that was.

Warily, he considered what the maturity of his tail portended. Surely he was on his way to being the first Elder of his species in a millennium, and along with that came, of course, immortality. Did the Womb realize this would happen? Did it have anything to do with his long forgotten mission? Baby stuck his head out of the picnic basket, looked around, climbed out, shuffled his way behind the fruit stand, lay down, stretched out his extremities and started to *eat*.

Chapter 4

Wil emerged from his room for the last time. He saw that the sky was gloomy and overcast. He didn't do well on days like this. He always felt depressed when the sun went into hiding.

He'd said goodbye to his pa and ma last night. His two brothers weren't interested in his affairs, so goodbyes weren't needed. He felt he was leaving very little behind. His pa and ma had income from the large boarding house that had been in his Italian father's family for generations. Both of his older brothers still lived at home with no signs of wanting to take a bride. He knew his pa and ma would be looked after.

He sure would miss his ma. He favored her with his bright clear blue eyes. She was Irish, from a big family. He had hopes that someday he'd have a family full of healthy little boys and pretty little girls. He thought of all the time he'd wasted on his halfhearted courting of Lexa, the only daughter of an Italian family from a town neighboring Boontown, where his family lived.

More accurately, it had been a case of her courting him. She was a big unfortunate-looking girl, very domineering, with a negative habit of constantly belittling him. *Let's face it, she's a beast.* With him out of the running, he was sure she'd have little chance of another suitor. Why he'd allowed himself to get involved was beyond him. His desire to have a family sure had overruled his common sense.

Wil Capaccino was a quiet young man of twenty one years, of medium height, but well-built with strong shoulders. His expression was sober and guileless, but when he smiled and those beautiful blue eyes lit up, he could melt the hardest anvil. Of course he was completely unaware of this. He thought himself a fair carpenter and wasn't afraid to put in a hard day of work. And he was funny. He loved to make his friends laugh. He'd miss them.

He'd saved much of his wages from the last few years, only spending on presents for his ma and the occasional outing with Lexa when he couldn't avoid her. His ma's life had been hard; caring for both of Wil's grannies, the boarders, his brothers and his pa. He'd miss her. But he knew it was time. If he was to make a stab at finding a full life for himself, he had to leave the small, predominantly Italian town he grew up in.

Norris County wasn't big enough to escape the wrath of Lexa's Neanderthal brothers so he thought he'd strike out for Sussex County. A man could find plenty of work in the farms that surrounded the country towns. Hopefully, he'd find the right little valley where he could buy himself a few acres of good bottom land and settle down.

Saddling up his mare, Maggie, he checked his bedroll and camping supplies. He wondered if he should bring another blanket, for winter hovered right around the corner. Dismissing the necessity, he mounted Maggie, tipped his hat to his boyhood home and took off down the trail.

Events chugged along nicely for Netty as the end of the brutal winter neared. Not a single day went by for want of food to eat. Netty loved to go down into the deep root cellar she'd paid to have dug last summer. It was extra-large to handle all the labors of her canning. She felt rich and accomplished. Her shelves gleamed with glass, reflecting the beautiful deep colors produced by her fertile field and the vigorous plants that had produced amazing sizes and quantities of fruits and vegetables never before seen in this part of the country, or maybe even the world. She prayed that the seeds she'd collected for next season's planting would be just as prolific.

As the news of her successful farming spread, townspeople showed up at her door looking to trade goods for a sample of her home-cooked goodies. As a result the cabin looked much warmer and more cheerful. Bouncy chintz curtains at her windows, braided hooked rugs on the polished wooden floor. A stunning quilt lay across her bed; a gift for herself that she'd purchased from the church ladies on her last trip into town. She now owned her own horse and wagon; a huge extravagance, but a necessary one. She found it so much easier to carry her wares into town to sell rather than risk someone catching sight of Baby. It was bad enough that she took chances whenever she traded her crops and pies for repairs or construction around the cabin. Baby had developed a set of horns that were becoming more pronounced. Mature and elegant, they took on the sheen and hardness of solid gold. They sprouted up in such a growth pattern that they were growing through his crown of crystal antlers. When she stroked them, they felt warm and alive, way too tempting for many local hunters. She was afraid Baby might catch someone's fancy and, when she turned her back, he'd be gone.

Her relationship with Baby grew closer than ever. They had stayed lost in their own world for most of the winter. Baking by day and enjoying the fire, curled up on Baby's straw bed near the fireplace that roared all day into the night. There had been only one strange incident.

It was the afternoon before the Sabbath. She'd dragged a rug outside to beat it over by the woodpile, sneezing as the dust rose from the rug to tickle her nose. Baby had joined her, lying in the snow doing his normal *eating*. It seemed to be a common practice. She now took it for granted, realizing it must be necessary. Baby said he was eating and she believed him. She figured it must have something to do with the sun. Baby once sent whispers and golden rainbow colors to her mind, attempting to explain something about molecular biology, kinetic energy and the evolution of organic chemistry and electrical current conversions. The terms were so foreign, she gave up trying to understand.

Completing the beating of the rug, she'd carried it back into the cabin. As she gathered up another rug for the woodpile, she'd heard a knock at the door. Opening it, she'd stepped out to the stoop to see a trapper holding up a bloodied, wriggling snow rabbit. The rabbit's legs were horribly broken, evidence of a cruel steel trap. The trapper had offered the rabbit in exchange for some dinner and lodging in her brand new barn.

Before she could respond, she'd felt the familiar pressure accompanied by the smell of sulfur. Glancing worriedly to the woodpile behind the trapper's back, she saw Baby's glorious tail at attention and the strange frightening membrane protruding. Before the trapper could question the sudden strange smell, his crippled rabbit had jumped from his arms and quickly scampered down the road. Netty had quickly shooed the trapper away with a gift of a golden raspberry pie.

As soon as she'd seen him off down the road, she'd gathered Baby up in her overcoat and run to the cabin, quickly bolting it from the inside, her heart beating uncontrollably. She'd shaken her head at Baby. How to explain the danger and risk if Baby were not more careful displaying his more flamboyant talents?

Her mind had flashed with rainbows and whispers. "I am Elder now, Sister. Such is my imperative." *Elder? Has Baby gotten old?*

"Baby, how old *are* you? Where are your parents, your mommy and daddy?"

"No parents, only Brothers and Sisters. I do not know old. I will be always."

Baby's cryptic comments had only befuddled her. No matter how she asked, she couldn't get clarification. So, begging Baby to be more aware, she'd dropped the subject. She needed to get to the barn to milk the cows after collecting them from the fields.

Netty's new pride and joy was her fledgling herd of Jerseys. If four could be considered a herd. She had great hopes for spring calving. She would love to add butter, cheese and milk to her deliveries.

Baby was an unexpected help at harvest time, but she could sure use some extra hands. It was clear she was spreading herself thin. Netty asked Baby to remain in the cabin while she milked the cows.

She reached for her boots and overcoat. Bending down to put on the boots, she winced, feeling her tailbone ache as if it was badly bruised. *Feels a bit worse,* she thought, having first noticed the pain about a week ago. Straightening up, she buttoned her overcoat and prepared to tramp through the snow along the winding path that the herd had created by moving back and forth from the field to the barn.

The cold felt particularly bitter. Netty thought she should have brought the herd in earlier, but she'd dawdled, trying to conserve the herd's hay, stored safely in the new barn. The more they grazed under the snow, the longer the hay would last. As the little herd spotted her, they came running. They knew her appearance meant they were going back to their warm barn to be milked.

As they ran ahead, Netty noticed a flicker of light through the trees. Was someone camping on her property? She didn't mind as long as they passed through quickly. She had to wonder if they were gypsies. Now that the farm was becoming prosperous, she was bound to become a target for petty theft. Glancing back at the herd, she saw they'd disappeared from sight, well on their way back to the barn. *Oh well*, she thought. *I better check this out.*

She absently regretted not bringing her Winchester with her. Shrugging to herself, she carefully made her way through four-foot snowdrifts to the woods on the other side of the field. Climbing the split-rail fence, she listened for voices, trying to get an idea of what she was up against. She found the silence ominous.

Creeping ever so slowly, she got nearer and nearer until she realized the light was not from a fire, but a small kerosene lantern sitting on a rock. A horse snorted at her approach: very skittish, very skinny.

As Netty approached the remains of a fire, she kneeled down to feel the burnt embers: cold. And very wet. She looked up and saw a fir tree standing over the fire. *Who would be so foolish as to build a fire under a snow-laden tree?*

Standing, she silently surveyed the clearing, her eyes coming to rest on a large, dark lump in the snow. Cautiously, she approached the mound. She startled, suppressing a scream as the lump moved. It emitted a hack and a cough. It was a man; what appeared to be a solitary man. She could handle that. Gently, she poked him with her foot.

"Hello there, sir." Receiving no reply, she wondered if he was injured. Kneeling down, she took his arm and gently rolled him over.

He was sick, that was for sure. She could see the fever: his cheeks flushed, his body shaking with chills, ice coating his dark mustache and beard. He appeared to be youngish, but all further examination would have to wait. If she left him out here, she doubted he and his horse would make it. *Well*, she thought, *if I could cure little creatures as a child, why not a big one, now that I am a grown woman?*

Netty rose and slowly crept over to the mare. "Easy, girl, easy." She slowly held out her hand displaying a piece of carrot from her overcoat, a cache she kept stored in her pockets for the cows. The mare crept forward and greedily snatched the carrot. Netty released her lead rope from the branch it was hitched to.

She looked around for the mare's tack, spotting her blanket but no saddle. *How can that be?* Locating the mare's bridle was not easy either. For some reason, it lay in the stranger's hands. *Perhaps he tried to leave the woods before he got sick*, she thought.

She noticed the absence of a firearm. *Who is this man?* He surely wasn't prepared to survive. Walking the mare over to the stranger, she ordered her to stay. Pulling the stranger into a sitting position, she grasped his hands and tried to pull him up to a standing position. She realized this wasn't going to be easy. She had to make him stand so she could get him over the saddle blanket. She could then lead his mare to the cow path and back to her cabin.

Fighting gamely, she finally got him upright, but couldn't get the mare to hold still long enough to lean him against her side and boost him up. Once in his delirium he muttered the name Maggie. *That must be his wife*, she thought. *She must be very worried.* Netty was determined that Maggie would get her husband back in good condition. The thought of her being party to making another woman a widow upset her. Especially a woman as young as Maggie must be.

Continuing her struggle, Netty soon realized she needed help. The closest farm was five miles away. She didn't think the stranger would survive being exposed to the elements for the amount of time it would take her to bring back assistance. She decided to risk bringing Baby back to help her. It was the only way.

By now, Netty was sweating with exertion, her clothes soaking wet. She worried about getting sick herself, something she couldn't afford. Netty let her memory wander as she hurried down the cow path to the cabin. It was very odd, but she couldn't recall having had so much as a sniffle since arriving at the farm. She'd frequently caught all manner of illnesses in the last decade. Being big and fat certainly hadn't helped. Back then, even her heart had consistently had palpitations. Funny how she'd only just realized that the palpitations had stopped. It must be because she'd lost so much weight. She recognized that her muscles felt like rocks. *That is what constant work does to you*, she thought proudly as she reached the barn where the cows waited to be let inside.

Bursting into the cabin, she called out to Baby.

"Sister upset?" her mind queried.

Grabbing one of her own sweaters, she quickly wrapped Baby up, explaining what she needed.

"A Brother in the woods." The whisper sounded curious. Grabbing Baby's hand, she opened the cabin door. Baby stopped, disengaged himself from the sweater and slipped his tiny golden hand back into hers, whispering in her mind.

"Come, Sister."

Mystified, Netty realized she'd never seen Baby outside in the snow for long. She accepted the fact that he didn't feel the cold in quite the same way as she did. But it was night now, and freezing. Having no time left to ponder on the latest Baby surprise, she swept them over to the barn where the herd still waited. She let them in, securing the door. They'd have to help themselves to the hay tonight. And milking would come much later than usual.

Netty and Baby hurried back to the field, searching for the stranger. He was right where Netty had left him, his mare nuzzling his face. Netty looked at Baby expectantly. Nothing happened. She then took Baby's glorious tail and held it up in the air; still nothing. *Why does Baby not fix him?* Looking into Baby's swirling eyes for an answer, she felt pressure in her mind as the golden aura flashed and the whisper shouted.

"*It is forbidden.*"

Ouch. Netty felt shock and frustration, rubbing her forehead. *Since when does a whisper shout?* Thinking Baby must have his reasons, she decided she wouldn't question why. That question would have to wait for a more opportune time. She would just care for the stranger the old fashioned way.

This time, pulling him up on his feet was easier with Baby's help. Baby held the mare's reins as Netty soothed her and levered the stranger up across the saddle blanket. They slowly worked their way through the snow back to the cabin.

Arriving safely, Netty slipped the stranger from the saddle blanket, asking Baby to take the mare to the barn and bed her down with the herd, making sure he fed and watered them all. That was a big responsibility for Baby as Netty had never asked him to do anything on his own without her being nearby. Glancing back toward the barn, she saw little Baby shuffling and bobbing along as he led the huge mare by her reins to the barn. *What a sight*, thought Netty, her heart swelling with laughter and affection.

Grasping the stranger under his arms, she yanked him into the cabin a few inches at a time. Pulling him over to Baby's straw mat, she laid him down carefully, noting the ice and snow were melting from his face. *A nice face*, she thought in passing.

Pulling off his overcoat and shirt, she decided to remove everything. Quickly she took a towel and rubbed him down. His body trembled with chills. She modestly toweled around his manhood as Baby startled her, peering around her skirt.

"Wet Brother on my bed, Sister," her mind whispered.

"Yes, Baby, this man is very sick. You must heal him. We can then send him home to his wife who misses him and is probably very worried." No whisper came to her head.

She covered the stranger with a blanket and put a pot on the fire to start a healing broth. While the broth simmered, she went to the barn to check on the livestock and do the milking.

Entering the cabin after her chores, she quickly poured the fragrant broth into a bowl for the stranger. While it cooled, she took stock. He had no firearm, no money (she'd thoroughly inventoried his belongings) and few of the supplies that would normally be necessary to survive in this weather. She also discovered a huge swelling over his right ear. As she undressed him, she discovered that his left side sported a huge black and blue mark which she knew would be tender to the touch. She began to wonder if he'd been bushwhacked and robbed. If so, the fact that he lived showed he was well-favored by Lady Luck. Usually they would just shoot their victims and take everything.

Noticing the broth was now cool, she carefully tried to spoon it into the man's mouth. It was a toss-up as to what received the most: the man's mouth or his neck. But his shivering seemed to have abated. She put the bowl aside, realizing he might be in better condition than she'd at first thought.

Covering the man tightly, she went for another blanket, hearing him murmur, "Maggie," as she tucked him in.

As she watched him dozing more fitfully, she realized she must now take the time to pin down Baby. Tired of putting it off for so long, she prepared to formulate the questions. The appearance of the stranger had merely exacerbated her need to know. She glanced at Baby, who made himself comfortable on a rug in front of the fire, his mysterious tail glinting as it lay wrapped around his chubby abdomen. Sitting down next to him, she took a deep breath and asked, "Baby, where do you come from?"

"Oolaha." The whisper was casual.

"Oolaha, what is Oolaha? Is that a name? The town near your woods?"

"I do not understand, Sister," the whispered aura stated.

"I asked you where you came from. Where did your family live?"

"Oolaha," the whisper repeated.

Netty, feeling frustrated, changed the subject. Taking Baby's hands in hers, she looked directly into his amazing eyes. "Why do you not want to heal him?"

Softly, hesitantly, the whisper said, "It is forbidden."

"Who has forbidden it?"

"The Elders, the Womb."

"But you told me you were an Elder, Baby. And you healed me."

"A grave error, Sister." The aura of golden colors in her mind flashed intermittently.

"A mistake, Baby? I am a mistake?"

"No, no," the whisper protested. "Sister is my Sister! Sister will be my Sister forever. Just Baby and Sister, forever and forever and forever and forever and forever and forever," the whisper sang, golden colors so bright her mind flinched.

"Shush. There, there, Baby, it will be fine." Netty could not follow what Baby had said, but it had clearly upset him. So she gave up. Baby filled her new life with such happiness, and she filled her own life with such hard satisfying work that she decided the mystery could wait. Checking on the stranger one last time, she scooped Baby into her arms and wearily went off to bed. As her eyes shut, she felt Baby cuddle up to her tummy, as always. Closing her eyes, her last thought echoed with praise and thanks to God for gifting her with such a precious creature: her confusing, beautiful Baby.

The next morning, Netty rose quickly, instructing Baby to stay in the bedroom for today, trying to impress upon him the necessity for secrecy. She quickly lit the fireplace and started a kettle for hot water. Checking on the stranger, she saw he was still sleeping. Quietly, she tiptoed back to her bedroom to change. As she washed, she looked at herself in the mirror and indulged in a little daydreaming.

The stranger's handsomeness had woken some mighty strange feelings within her, even in his present condition. She realized he was probably married, but wondered how attractive a man might find her. *Oh, silly,* she thought. Laughing to herself, she dipped her washcloth in the water, wringing it out. She reached down to scrub her bottom as she wondered what to make for lunch.

"*Ow, my gosh.*" Trembling, she reached behind her and felt something emerging from her tailbone. It was a lump the size of an apple. Fearfully, she pressed down on it, expecting it to burst. No, it felt solid but spongy and swollen. She felt some mild pain but, with the help of a hand mirror, she didn't see any redness. Nervously, she worried about getting sick. She just couldn't afford it; so much had to be done on the farm, even in winter. Only a minor miracle had helped her manage to accomplish this much on her own. Ruefully, she realized her good health might fail her, putting an end to her good fortune.

Her mind now preoccupied, she said goodbye to Baby with a hug and returned to the other room to discover the stranger conscious and beginning to move. Turning his head toward the noise of her bedroom door shutting, he stared at her.

"Hello. Who are you? Where am I?"

Netty stood speechless as the stranger's unwavering gaze invited an explanation. His eyes shot guileless ice-blue beacons at her, creating an unexpected moment of vulnerable intimacy. Transfixed and a bit flustered, she brought a chair to the straw bed and sat down before him.

"My name is Netty Doyle. I found you in my field. You were unconscious and feverish so I brought you and your mare to my cabin. Your mare is in my barn. She is safe and well fed." Netty shifted uncomfortably in her chair, the stranger's gaze causing her to fidget. "I found very little at your camp site. Perhaps you could tell me who you are?"

The stranger struggled to sit up. Blushing beet red, he turned to her. "Where are my clothes, madam?"

Netty blanched, bounding to the other side of the fireplace to remove them from the rope line where she hung the laundry in the winter. Apologizing, she returned to the stranger and set his clothes next to him on the bed. She dropped her eyes before addressing him again.

"Who are you, sir?"

The stranger smiled, a lazy grin belying the formal tone of his voice. "Forgive me, Mrs. Doyle, my manners are not normally so poor. I must thank you for rescuing me. My name is Wil. Wil Capaccino. My family hails from Boontown in Norris County."

Netty cringed visibly at the mention of Norris County. Mr. Capaccino seemed not to recognize her name. Doyle was a common

Irish name, but Robert was well known throughout the county. With visible relief, she noticed Mr. Capaccino's eyelids sinking. Within minutes, his soft snores resounded through the cabin.

The morning passed quickly with Mr. Capaccino waking periodically to take some broth before falling back asleep. Netty itched to hear more from her accidental guest. She could tell from the cut of his clothes and the calluses on his strong hands that his living was forged by hard work. The manner of his speech showed him to be educated, but of the country classes. Just like her. It somehow made her feel more comfortable. She was not a huge judge of character, but she sensed an honesty and sweetness in him.

Netty wondered how long it would take him to gain his strength. By the looks of his health, she thought he'd be up and on his way in a few days. Some of her gratifying meals were bound to help.

Netty's main concern centered around Baby. If he must stay cooped up in her bedroom for so long, he'd surely be getting hungry. He needed to get outside to eat. Thinking of Baby eating made her remember dinner. She would make her favorite bean stew with fresh butter milk biscuits. And, if they had enough flour left, she'd make an apple cobbler, just the way her mama had. After all, they didn't have company for dinner very often. Well, never, actually. Smiling, she bustled around the kitchen until the sound of Mr. Capaccino's voice drew her to his bedside.

"Eh, Mrs. Doyle, I need, uh, I mean I need to, ah, where is your outhouse?"

"Mr. Capaccino. You are much too weak to go out in the snow just yet. I can prepare something that will make do." Crossing the room, she picked up a blanket and returned to his bedside. She looked down on his face, bright red with embarrassment, and said, "Mr. Capaccino, I have already seen everything you have." Handing him a jar, she held the blanket up as he relieved himself. Taking the jar from his hand, she went to the door and dumped it off the stoop.

After preparing a hot bath for Mr. Capaccino in her pig iron tub in the corner of the cabin, she helped him rise from the straw bed. She saw he was still unsteady, but was able to creep to the tub with her help.

"Mrs. Doyle, if you please?"

"Of course, Mr. Capaccino." Modestly turning away, she found busy work in the kitchen. "Mr. Capaccino, I would be very pleased if you could join me for some tea and cornbread muffins when you are finished there."

"It would be my pleasure, madam. Something sure smells good."

Netty hurriedly set the table for the two of them. She slipped into her bedroom to give her radiant lush hair a quick adjustment, sweeping it up once more into a ponytail. Running to her bed, she lifted the covers to find Baby relaxing.

"Sister's face is red. Does Sister need my help?"

"No, Baby, everything is fine. I will be talking to our guest until bedtime. Will you please stay here? This is where you will be safe." Netty then remembered. "Baby, do you need to eat? I can try to figure a way to sneak you out the door?"

"No, Sister, tomorrow will be fine." And with that, Netty skipped out to the kitchen.

She came upon Mr. Capaccino sitting patiently at the kitchen table, smiling expectantly at her. Her stomach did a flip flop as she quickly joined him. He'd shaved his beard and regained some healthy color in his cheeks, making him look like an eager young boy. But, as Netty well knew, he was clearly a man. Netty slowly poured the tea and passed the plate of muffins.

"Mr. Capaccino, can you now please tell me what happened to you? What were you doing on my land?"

"Mrs. Doyle, can you find it in your heart to call me Wil? I fear you know me much better than I intended."

"Of course, Mr., ah, Wil, and you must call me Netty," she said shyly, unable to meet his eyes.

"Well, Netty, I was just passing through. Thought I would take a shortcut to town. My mare and I ran out of provisions. I do believe we became a tad lost. Seeing a fire through the woods, I thought to hail my fellow travelers." He shook his head ruefully. "Next time, I sure plan to exercise more caution. The ambush didn't take long. As

I rode into the clearing, I got yanked off my horse so fast I jerked the reins right out of her mouth. They sat me on the ground with a rifle on me as they divvied up my money and gear. I think the plan was to take my horse and shoot me, but they were frightened off by a voice in the nearby field. I assume that was you, Netty. One of the bandits clubbed me in the face as he ran. Luckily, they left my horse and a lantern. The fire was of no use. Having placed it under a snow-covered tree, the heat loosened the snow and quickly smothered the flame. We survived the night praying for your voice again, hoping you would find us. I do not know how long I was out, but my wish came true. You saved us, Netty."

"Oh, Wil, how terrible." Placing her hands over his, she sighed, "And your poor wife, Maggie, she must be beside herself."

"Maggie? You know about Maggie?" Wil burst out laughing. He was laughing so hard, Netty jerked her hand back in surprise.

"No, no, Netty." Still laughing, Wil announced, "I am so sorry, I am not married to Maggie. She is my horse. She *is* my girl, though."

With unexpected relief, Netty refilled their cups and got up to stir the evening stew. Attempting to hide her embarrassment, she changed the subject. "Wil, would you care to check on Maggie after dinner tonight? I have to go to the barn to milk the cows anyway." Netty had neglected to turn them out to pasture that morning, being preoccupied with her guest.

"I gratefully accept your offer, Netty. And, if you do not mind, I think I need to lie down now." As Wil rose, Netty rushed to help him. Waving her off, he made his way carefully to the bed on his own. Easing himself down, Netty heard him take a deep breath.

"I must be really under the weather. I had the dangest dreams last night. I dreamed I saw a golden deer, or was it a cat? What a fantastic creature. Its eyes contained rainbows, Netty. Is that not a crazy dream?"

"That is what happens when you are sick with delirious tremors." Netty held her breath. Wil didn't question her explanation. *He will only be here for another day or so, then be on his way,* Netty told herself. Her secret would be safe.

Later, over a long hearty dinner, Wil and Netty got to know each other. Netty explained how she'd inherited the family farm, omitting the gruesome details, while Wil shared his dreams for his future. After dinner, Netty allowed Wil to clear the table. He seemed to be rapidly gaining strength. The dishes were soon stacked and put away.

"Wil, are you ready for a trip to the barn?"

"Yes, madam. If you do not mind, I thought I would look around and see if I could repay your fine hospitality with some work."

"There is no shortage of work to be done on this farm, Wil." Netty laughed, unashamed. Slipping into their overcoats, they headed to the barn.

"Sometimes I think it is time to hire some help. But I do not think I can afford to do that unless I expand my baking capacity to pay for it. There is only so much you can do with one oven." Helping each other through the snow, they laughed together as they slipped in their heavy boots. Stopping in the doorway of the barn, Wil raised their lantern. He stared into Netty's eyes.

"Gosh, you sure are beautiful. The color of your eyes cannot be real. They look like spun gold. How can that be?"

"It sounds like you are still delirious, Mr. Capaccino." Laughing, Netty put him off. She wasn't used to compliments and wondered if Wil was being forward. As wonderful as it felt to be in his company, she'd little experience with men. (Her husband certainly didn't count.) Anyway, she knew she couldn't have Wil around for long. It would only invite disaster for Baby.

Showing Wil around the barn, he pointed out many small improvements that could be made. He was thrilled to see Maggie. She didn't hesitate to help herself to the sweet hay belonging to the Jerseys. They were completely unconcerned by her presence. After watering and milking the livestock, Wil helped Netty bring in the milk, depositing a large portion in her butter churn.

As Netty churned away, she learned more about him, his family, the unfortunate Lexa, and his boyhood town. She felt a bond with his story. His background was much like hers: a poor, honest, working class family, a closeness to his mother. He was smarter than her, she could see that. She felt a need in him, a searching or striving for a place he could be happy. A place he could put his feet up; his sanctuary. His ideas for increasing productivity and simplifying her workload impressed her with their simplicity and creativity. The idea tempted her, all right.

Saying goodnight to each other, Netty got ready for bed. As she undressed, she looked critically at herself. She was quite striking with her golden eyes and long gold and brown hair. The changing of her eyes had happened so gradually, she'd just accepted it without much question. Her hands slipped down to her bottom where the growth was becoming elongated and supple. It was easy to hide under her skirts for now. Yes, for now. Would it continue to grow? She no longer feared the growth would kill her. But she did fear the change it might bring to her body. And of course, how would she expose it to anyone? She refused to let anyone observe the freak she might become. That was unthinkable.

Before she snuffed out her candle, she played with Baby on the bed. She liked to tickle his tummy. He didn't have the capability to laugh, but he loved to stroke her own face with his elongated leathery fingers. He loved tangling his golden crown of antlers in her hair. When they became too tangled, she would pick him up by his feet and shake him loose. He couldn't get enough of it. Quietly, she soothed him down for sleep, murmuring love sounds to him as she drew the warm quilt over them, blowing out the lantern.

The next morning was sunny and warmer. Clearly, the winter was coming to an end. Her orchard would soon be sprouting leaves. Her tilling and planting would start all over. Bread must bake, pies to make, butter to churn, and winter repair money to earn.

Her little herd still needed her attention, immediately.

Wil hovered over the morning fire as she entered the kitchen.

"You look good this morning, Wil. I mean, you look recovered." Her face flamed with self-consciousness.

"I feel good. How 'bout I help you turn out the herd? I can check the campsite in the woods and see if anything was left behind." Wil sounded eager and she needed to start getting some work accomplished.

"All right, we can bring lunch with us. I need to check my fence posts to assess what the snow brought down."

"Netty, why don't we bring a few tools with us? I can fix any damage we find."

"Oh, Wil, I would be so grateful. Repairing the fences takes so long. I usually do not find the time until the fields have been planted. Now I shall not have to worry about the cows wandering." Netty was secretly relieved that Baby would also have plenty of time to get outside to do his *eating.*

Netty packed a big lunch for them in a basket, adding large jars of fresh milk. Slipping in an extra generous slice of her rhubarb pie, she was reminded she must get back to her baking. A large order awaited and needed to be completed within a few days if she wanted to get it to town on time. She really didn't have any more time to fritter away as she got to know her houseguest, pleasant though it was.

Loading up the tools from the barn, Wil tied their burden across Maggie's saddle blanket. *What a relief not to be forced to drag everything to the field.* There'd be plenty to do once they arrived. Much would be accomplished if they were fresh, and of course, having Wil's strong shoulders would make the job go twice as fast. They set off for the pasture, following the well-worn cow path.

Netty surveyed the pasture as the cows filtered in. She noticed the gate needed some reinforcing, its list was now quite pronounced. Scanning down the field, she counted the downed trees. Naturally, many of them had landed on her fence, damaging the rails.

"Do not worry, Netty, I can have some of those saplings trimmed out and that mess cleaned up in no time. I think we will be up here working for most of the day, though."

They set to work. What would have taken Netty days of struggle, took no time at all with Wil's help. She admired his skill. Everything he touched turned out perfectly. It sure was good to have a professional on the job.

The day wore on, with Netty and Wil only stopping for a very late lunch. While Wil gulped down her rhubarb pie, he commented on an idea he wanted her to consider. His plan should increase her oven space, if she allowed him to knock a hole in the kitchen wall to enlarge the room. He would also require most of the fieldstone from the pile she was accumulating for her boundary markers. It would increase her baking output fourfold, and she'd have much more room in the kitchen for her supplies. Netty loved the sound of his plan, but the ground-breaking would have to wait until the weather warmed up. In the meantime, Wil could help her get the fields ready for planting, maybe clear another field for a new crop. Netty's thoughts swam with the possibilities. Wil sounded very ambitious. *But Baby, what about Baby?*

"I do not know, Wil." Netty sounded reluctant. "I do not think I have the room to take on a fulltime live-in hand."

"Netty, do not worry, I can bunk in with Maggie and the cows. The worst of the cold will soon be over." He sounded so hopeful.

"Let me think about it, Wil."

"Okay, Netty." Standing, Wil brushed off the crumbs from his meal. "I think I will try to find the bandits' campsite. Hopefully, some of my things might still be around." Wil tramped off through the snow, leaving Netty alone with the cows.

Wil puzzled over the abrupt change in Netty's attitude. He would sure love to work here. He found Netty sweet and earnest. Her cooking was fantastic and she was darn easy to look at. He sensed a reluctance to talk about her marriage. She kept mum about her husband. *Where is he?* She was perfectly clear about the farm being hers, but vague about her actual marriage status. And no children. He thought that was odd since she mentioned she'd been married for years. Well, he best mind his own business and hope she decided to take him on as a hand. A woman like her shouldn't be alone this far from town, anyway.

Hoping for the best, he arrived at the bandits' campsite. Not much remained except the cold ashes of their campfire. Scanning the area, he noticed they had dropped his saddle. What a relief to recover it, perfectly molded to Maggie's broad back. He'd have had a hard time with her if he'd lost it. Bareback gets mighty uncomfortable with stowed gear and riding over long distances. Since they'd robbed him of all his savings, he had to find work to replace everything.

Meeting Netty had been fortunate in more than one way. That is, if he could convince her to take him on. Unfortunately, she didn't seem to be the kind of lady that could be talked into things. She had a spine. He sure admired all the hard work she'd expended in putting the farm back in order; a monumental task. *She sure is some woman.*

Wil returned to the cow pasture, observing Netty rounding up the Jerseys. He loaded the tools onto Maggie's back then, running to the gate, he held it open as Netty shooed the herd through.

Walking back down the worn cow path, they noticed the temperature drop remarkably. The snow that had seemed soft and slushy this morning, now crunched and slipped under their feet. Their breath made gusty little clouds in front of them as they hurried to the barn. The Jerseys, sensing the barn was close, broke into a run, desiring as much as Netty and Wil to get out of the freezing cold.

As Netty and Wil approached the barn with Maggie, they saw the Jerseys milling and shoving each other out of the way to be the first at the door, their hooves clacking on a thin layer of ice formed from snowmelt dripping off the roof. Reaching past Netty to open the barn door, Wil took his eyes off Maggie as he held her reins. Maggie snickered as she was bumped by one of the cows, her hooves flailing on the ice. As Wil opened the barn door, down she went, screaming as she fell, the thud bone-shattering. Wil gasped, his eyes unbelieving as he stared at the devastating break. He dropped down to the ground, cradling Maggie's head as tears dropped from his anguished eyes to land on her steaming muzzle. Her eyes flared, wild with pain as Wil tried to calm her. He knew there was only one solution.

"Netty," he screamed between sobs. "*Get me your rifle.*" Netty moved as if to run, but stayed glued to her spot. "*Netty,*" Wil screamed again. Rising to run for the rifle himself, he turned to the stoop and felt shock course through him as he saw the strange creature from his dreams in all its golden glory. The creature's tail rose in the air and hovered. From the end of the tail emerged a fleshy bulbous hunk of something. As it wavered in the air, Wil was assailed with the smell of sulfur and the feeling of pressure on his chest.

"*What the heck?*" Wil screamed. He grabbed Netty and threw her to the ground, covering her with his body.

"Wil, get off me." Netty squirmed underneath him. Her heart beat frenetically at her breast with the shock of seeing Baby on the stoop. She'd expressly told him to be back inside well before nightfall.

"Sister, Wil and Maggie needed my help," the aura in her mind whispered, its susurrations swirling. "It is my mandate. I must heal."

Netty scrambled out from underneath Wil, running to the stoop as he rose to his feet to stare in shock at Maggie. *She was on her feet.* And, as they watched in disbelief, she calmly walked into the barn to join the Jerseys.

Quickly turning back to the stoop, Netty fearfully watched Wil crouch down in a defensive position, Baby tucked protectively in her arms. Before he could say a word, she rose and scampered into the cabin, slamming the door.

Wil stood dumbfounded. *What just happened?* He went to the barn to fill the water trough and examine Maggie. As he brushed her coat, he inspected her leg. *Should I question my eyes? Did I make a mistake?* No, that was crazy. He'd seen her pain with his own eyes. And he'd heard her screams. Looking into her placid eyes, it was as if nothing had happened. Left with no choice, he knew he must demand an explanation from Netty. He felt pretty sure the blame rested with that unnatural creature on her stoop. The same creature imagined in his dreams. Obviously, he must have caught a glimpse of it before while in his feverish state.

Wil let himself into the cabin, not seeing Netty. Softly, he knocked at her bedroom door. No answer.

"Netty," he called softly. "Please let me in. I think we had better talk about this." Slowly, the door cracked open and Netty swept into the room. Her eyes darted around, seeing nothing. She paced frantically around the kitchen until Wil grabbed her by the arms and sat her down. He could feel her trembling though her shawl.

"Netty, what happened? How can this be? Maggie's leg is healed. It looks like it was never broken. Netty, please talk to me."

"I am sorry, Wil." Netty chewed frantically on her lip. "I do not know what to say."

"What do you mean, you do not know what to say?" he shouted. "Why don't you start with that creature? What is it? Can it hurt you? Where did you get it?"

Netty remained silent as Wil stood over her, spouting questions. She could sense his effort to keep his anger in check, but for how long? She knew an explanation about Baby must be proffered, but she didn't know where or how to start. *How will he understand? Will he keep my secret?*

As Netty's thoughts whirled, Wil got down on his knees in front of her, taking her in his arms. "Netty, it is all right. We will work this out. Stop trembling now. We can figure this out together."

Netty, surprised by his tenderness, started to cry. She might be older than Wil, but she felt a kind of strength in him that she'd only felt before from her real papa, Mr. Woods. Between sobs, she told Wil the long story of her marriage betrayal, the isolation and rapes, the stolen gold coin, the discovery of her inheritance and of course, Baby. When she finished, she dried her tears, exhausted.

Wil rose, putting the kettle on for tea. Placing a cup in front of her, he sat down with a cup for himself, letting it cool. Netty didn't look up for fear of seeing condemnation in his eyes. No one said a word.

From the bedroom came a sound. They both looked to the bedroom door as it slowly opened. Out came Baby, shuffling and wobbling across the rug until he stood in front of Netty. He clambered up her skirt, taking his place on her lap. She softly stroked his golden fur as Wil stared.

"Is this creature your pet, Netty?" Wil's voice remained low, his tone soft and respectful, yet laced with incredulity. He suddenly felt a pressure in his head and saw pinpricks of rainbow lights, an aura in the back of his head making him dizzy.

"I am Brother," came a soft whisper. Wil looked directly at Baby in shock. Netty had left out this piece of information, it was just too unbelievable. "I am Elder now. Sister will be Elder soon," the whisper continued.

"He thinks you are his sister? That is him talking to me, is it not? Can you hear him talking to me?"

Netty cast her eyes down to Baby. "He talks to me when he wants. I do not hear what he says to you unless he wants me to. But Wil, what are you going to do?"

"Do about what, Netty? Oh, you mean Baby? Well, you clearly love him, he appears to be harmless, I *think*, that is. Oh, gosh, Netty, I do not know, there is nothing I can do anyway. What could I do? He saved Maggie. He has done good things for you. I would never do anything that would hurt you."

Jumping to her feet with Baby in her arms, she ran to Wil. She crushed him in an embrace, forcing Wil to circle his arms around them both. "Oh, thank you, thank you, Wil. You can stay now! I was so worried about you accidentally discovering Baby and not understanding, that I thought I must send you away, even though my heart rebelled. Please, you will stay now, won't you? I know you will be a huge asset to the farm."

"Just an asset to the farm, Netty?" Wil's eyes and mouth smiled at her, a question hanging in the air, unanswered. Netty lowered her eyes to give him her answer.

Chapter 5

Baby lay curled on the rug in front of the fireplace. He watched as Sister and Brother ate dinner together. He could feel emotion in the air. What a strange day. Sister's agitation had become pronounced during the last few days. As soon as he'd discovered the source, Brother, he'd decided to reveal himself. Baby didn't care for disrupted harmony. He sensed goodness in Brother, just as he had in Sister. He couldn't afford to have disharmony around Sister. She was changing. She would soon be an Elder, with all the responsibility that entailed. She needed his guidance, for it would change her life for good. Baby's contentment with Sister gave him a purpose. His mission had faded with his lost memory. He no longer expected the expiration that should have accompanied the Emergence of his offspring. Clearly, immortality was with him.

Netty, Baby and Wil adjusted nicely to each other's company. Wil slept out on the straw bed in the kitchen. He and Netty discussed the possibility of adding a small addition to the cabin as they built the new pie oven. It seemed a fine idea.

Wil rigged Maggie and the horse that pulled Netty's vegetable wagon to a plough to make their work easier. The plough turned over existing vegetation leaving a furrow to plant in. Better yet, it created two furrows at a time. Netty trailed behind to plop in the new seed and Baby smoothed over the new soil. They were very efficient. The orchard needed little work, except for removing the old canes from her raspberry and blackberry bushes. Wil had taken over responsibility for the Jerseys and did all the milking, which freed Netty up to keep ahead of her baking orders. In his spare time, Wil found enough needed repairs to keep him busy for the next few years.

Wil and Netty would sip tea and laugh, telling each other stories from their childhood well into the night after Netty's delicious dinners. Baby watched carefully from his spot on the rug. When they realized it was time for bed, Netty would call Baby to her, bend down to pick him up and give Wil a chaste kiss goodnight.

Wil wondered about Netty's reluctance to take the relationship any further. He compassionately chalked it up to her turbulent time with her husband. He was a patient man. They had their whole lives ahead of them. And he was nothing if not a gentleman. After all, he'd been raised by a God-fearing Catholic Irish mama who expected nothing less of him.

Netty and Baby lay down on the bed. Netty had yet to undress. She dreaded being reminded of her changes. She was clearly growing a tail, which looked just like Baby's. *Does that mean I can cure things as Baby can?* She didn't know how to even try. *Did Baby know I would change like this?* She'd tried to ask him, but he remained silent. Baby didn't talk much.

She wondered how this would affect her relationship with Wil. She was nuts about him and thought he felt the same. But she feared his revulsion. The changes to her body made her a freak. It might be too much for him. She didn't want to lose the part of him she did have. And what to do about the issue of Robert? She wondered why he'd not shown himself. She'd made a few discreet inquires and discovered that a wife's inheritance belonged to the husband too. Her timidity prevented her from inquiring about the process of divorce. She knew for sure that would bring Robert down on her to claim the farm. He'd admitted to murdering her mother and she knew he wouldn't hesitate to do the same to her. She thought it would be best if she left things as they were.

The spring moved into summer, then winter, and moved into spring again. They became the destination of choice for most of the town. Netty outgrew the new pie oven and was making plans with Wil for a huge new project; a bakery. It would be situated behind her old animal hospital, allowing them plenty of privacy at the cabin. And they would need it, because they'd made the monumental decision to hire some fulltime help for the new bakery.

Wil wanted to hire some field hands for his plan to expand their crops. Once these projects were completed, they both prayed their success might extend far enough to cover the extravagance of a truck. Other farmers had found the money to make the envied purchase, allowing their hard work to lighten with the new convenience. God knew what a boon a truck would be for the farm business.

Wil and Netty's relationship, surprisingly, didn't progress as he hoped. He tried not to let disillusion pull him down, but her behavior didn't seem normal to him. He knew her feelings for him ran deep. He often caught her studying him when she thought him unaware and would see such a look of longing. When she caught him looking at her, she'd blush and smile, making him feel hopeful.

They knew one another very well now. Sometimes, he'd start to say something and she would nod, finishing his sentence. They laughed together constantly, mostly over his silly grade school jokes. Her laughter, the best reward for a hard day of work. Although, of late, he sometimes noticed her voice contained a note of strain.

He loved his work on the farm. Seeing their progress and success delighted them both, making their lives very fulfilling. On the other hand, he knew Netty quietly fretted about her husband's possible claim on the farm. She haltingly explained the relationship between her mama and Mr. Woods. Wil took the news in stride. Many women found themselves in similar straits, marrying the next man that would have them, so as to give the child a name. Bastard children carried a stigma that was hard to shake. Netty was very lucky Mr. Woods had found a way to stay in her life. They might not know the reasons behind her mama's decision, but Mr. Woods had obviously loved her and provided for her. It was quite unfortunate that he'd inadvertently chosen a disreputable lawyer to represent him. Wil thought Netty might have a good case for fraud on her hands. When they had time, they planned to hire a lawyer in town to look into it for them.

Baby was another story. His relationship with Baby mirrored that of a big brother. Baby went nuts over Maggie. Wil would saddle up

Maggie early in the morning when he was turning out the Jerseys, and Baby would be right on his heels when he left the cabin. He had to struggle to keep up with Wil, his funny little shuffle and wobble a handicap. He sure was an eager little guy, though. Wil would lift him up on the saddle with him and off they'd go with the Jerseys, Baby clinging to the saddle horn with Wil's arm looped across his fat little tummy. Wil gave up counting how many times he'd rolled over in the night to discover Baby curled up under the covers with him.

Baby made no further effort to talk to him, though. Netty said it was normal; Baby didn't talk much.

Wil decided to make a move today. They never took any time off to go into town unless it was to bring produce, make pie deliveries or pick up supplies. Wil heard that one of the churches planned to host a Saturday supper with square dancing after dinner. There were bound to be some locals who made sure the men had a good supply of moonshine behind the church. Wil planned on inviting Netty to the supper this morning, and he launched into his proposal as Netty poured Wil's breakfast tea.

"Come on, Netty, it will be fun. We could sure use a break before spring planting starts."

Caught off guard by Wil's invitation, Netty's heart gave a trill of excitement. The thought of socializing had never occurred to her. Their affairs on the farm overwhelmed them so, keeping them busy, and she preferred to stick close to Baby, afraid to leave him alone. You could never tell when a stranger might stop by looking for some pies or a handout. She worried what might happen if they found no one home and decided to poke around.

"I do not know, Wil, can we really afford to take the time? I wanted to start moving the fieldstone up from the fields. We will soon be starting the foundation for the bakery."

"Netty, do not worry about that. Baby and I will start working on that on Sunday morning. I thought we would bring a load up after we turn out the Jerseys. We can get it done and still be finished in time for lunch."

"I am sure Baby's help will be overwhelming, but I do not know how I can afford the time." Looking at Wil's crestfallen face, Netty paused. Wil never complained about anything. She knew her reluctance to respond to his overtures portended an eventual rift between them. Her tail, fully mature, lay wrapped around her torso, hidden securely under her skirt. She hoped to delay a painful confrontation as long as possible. The thought of losing Wil because of her fear chilled her. Maybe if she said yes to the supper, Wil would be mollified for a while. Was it possible they might enjoy themselves?

"Well, maybe some time off would be good for us. I think Baby can hold down the fort until we get back." She smiled suddenly as Wil jumped up, grabbing her in a bear hug.

"I know that you will be the prettiest girl there."

As the day wore on, Netty's reservations returned, making her jumpy. Additional worries about the dance played on her mind. The fact that she'd never attended a dance before was the least of them.

Netty's unspoken insecurity revolved around the age difference between the two of them. She knew the young ladies of the town would use the dance as an opportunity to flirt and size up the single gentlemen. The supper presented the perfect atmosphere to look for strong, good-looking prospects, receptive to their mysterious signals, with the hope of spurring a courtship. Netty didn't want Wil to develop a wandering eye because of her unwillingness to explore a more intimate relationship. He didn't seem like the type, but she didn't know much about that side of him. She did know he'd always planned to marry and raise as many children as possible. That thought alone frightened her.

Having completed all of the day's chores, Netty washed up in her bedroom, Wil in the kitchen. As she slipped on a petticoat she sighed, never previously having had anywhere to go which merited wearing it. She noticed a large slit down the back of it, down to her tail. The slit was to facilitate ease in getting in and out of the voluminous garment. A drawstring allowed her to cinch it at her waist, holding the petticoat up. She would have to hold her tail tightly around her torso to prevent it from slipping through the slit and unraveling down her legs.

Slipping her best dress over her head, she looked at herself in her mirror. She looked just like she always did, except for the nervous flush. But she wanted to look special in some way for Wil, to mark the occasion. Feeling she needed an edge to compete with the youth of the other single ladies, she removed her ponytail, letting her lush, long hair fall down her shoulders. She noticed her hair had developed a golden sheen. *When did that happen?* Standing back, she discovered the appearance of a halo surrounding her. Well, she really didn't want to draw others' attention to herself, but it was the only edge she had.

Netty sat on her bed to say goodbye to Baby. Last night, they'd explained to him about their trip into town. If anyone knocked on the door, Baby was to crawl under the bed. They showed Baby how to lock the door from the inside and felt confident that the little guy would be safe. The trickle of town folk who had come out to her farm had fallen off since she'd started to bring her produce into town more regularly. With a feeling of confidence and anticipation, Netty slipped out of the bedroom to join Wil.

Wil finished dressing. His boots gleamed, his shirt was fully starched and his trousers pressed. They didn't do a thing to disguise his strong shoulders or lean, fit build. Turning, he watched Netty come from the bedroom. His heart ached with longing as she took his breath away. With her hair swinging down her back, she looked stunning. Her face gleamed: flushed and expectant. There seemed to be a golden glow radiating from her, leaving him speechless.

"Netty, you look beautiful," he whispered, going to her side. Netty blushed, looking down at her feet. Wil offered his arm and together they walked out to the barn to collect the wagon and start their ride into town.

The almost full moon lit their bumpy drive. Wil chattered excitedly all the way, Netty smiled and nodded but said little. When they arrived at the church, they hitched the wagon and loosened the rigging on the horse, who acted skittishly around the automobiles parked nearby. Entering the church hall, they made their way to a table where a popular tavern owner sat with his family. Quickly making space for Wil and Netty, they found themselves heartily welcomed.

Wil rose from the table to deliver their contribution, Netty's fabulous pies. Returning, he noticed various men glancing at Netty then nodding in his direction.

Most in town knew of Netty's husband, as some of his sisters still ruled the social scene. But these county folks were farmers and shopkeepers with their families. He felt assured he wouldn't have any trouble, being from out of town. The thing everyone in these parts respected most was hard work. Everyone greatly admired Netty's labor, even envied her for all she'd accomplished. Unfortunately, Wil had not counted on the speculation about his relationship with her. Some might consider it improper if they knew he slept in the house, instead of the barn. The last thing he wanted to do was cause Netty grief after he'd pressured her to come to the dance. He certainly didn't want to create a scandal that would hurt their business. Noticing more glances and whispers, he began to think of the supper and dance as a mistake.

Hurrying back to the table with two plates of food, he sat across the table from Netty and joined the boisterous conversation. As the evening wore on, the laughter at the table grew louder. Wil noticed the men casually slipping out the back door and returning with mugs brimming with what he could only guess was spirits. From time to time, the shopkeepers who often purchased Netty's wares stopped by with their wives to pay respect to her. Wil noticed the wives exhibited a stiffness in their greetings. Maybe it was his imagination. Perhaps they were just jealous of Netty's prettiness. She sure stood out in this crowd.

Netty herself flushed with pleasure, having a great time. She laughed more than she could remember ever having done before. Some of the business owners she'd previously targeted unsuccessfully, due to their loyalty to their current suppliers, asked her to stop by next week. She responded, happily introducing them to Wil and setting up a date and time. Her dinner was delicious, but, glancing at Wil, she saw he'd barely touched his plate. Puzzled, she smilingly reached for his hand across the table. She got a big, sweet smile in return. At a sideways glance from their host, he hurriedly withdrew his arm. *What is going on?* she wondered. *Has someone said something about me to Wil?*

Netty's attention shifted over to the men clearing space for the dance floor. The fiddle players entered and were in the corner tuning up. Oh, such fun. It would be the first time they would hold each other and dance. Netty observed young ladies tossing flirtatious glances at the men gathered near the back door.

She wanted to go to the outhouse before the dancing started. She cursed herself for not considering her needs carefully enough when she'd agreed to come. She would need a fair amount of time to safely secure her tail before she could return to the hall. Motioning to Wil, she asked him to accompany her to the door. Happy to be needed, he assisted Netty through the crush of laughing townspeople. Agreeing that he'd wait with the men enjoying their spirits, Netty made her way to the outhouse.

Waiting for Netty, Wil noticed the other men grinning at him. He felt uneasy, but chose to ignore it. He thought it best that, when Netty returned, they take their leave.

"So buddy, you getting any of that?" asked one grinning fool, clearly deep in his cups. The other men laughed as Wil turned his eyes on them. "She sure is a looker and those older ones really know what they're doing. We hear you might be doing some hiring out your way. That include any benefits?" The crowd thought the comment hilarious as they broke up laughing, holding their sides, trying unsuccessfully not to spill their precious spirits.

Wil balled his fists, ready for a fight, when he heard a scream down the path to the outhouse. Running as fast as he could, he saw Netty on the ground with some drunk assaulting her. He also noticed, unbelievably, that Baby had followed them to the dance, as he could clearly see his tail in the melee. Yanking the drunk off Netty, he punched him in the face, knocking him out cold. Wil scooped a sobbing Netty into his arms, looking around wildly for Baby. He needed to get Netty to the wagon. He didn't want any of the other drunks coming to investigate. He would then come back for Baby. He knew the urgency of secrecy. No one could discover their little creature. God knew what hell could break out.

Wil hurriedly deposited Netty in the wagon. Her face streaked with tears, she cried hysterically.

"Shush, Netty, I am here. Nobody will hurt you now." Wil held her in his arms, kissing and stroking her beautiful hair. As he slowly rocked her, she calmed down, her sobbing abating. "Netty, I have to go back to find Baby. He is out back. He must have followed us from the farm." Grabbing a blanket from the back of the wagon, he climbed down to search for Baby. Netty started screaming, "No, Wil, you cannot leave me!"

Gosh, she is terrified, Wil thought. "Netty, Baby is back there unprotected. I have to find him." Suddenly, he felt pressure in his head accompanied by flashes of a golden aura.

The whisper came softly, "Brother, you can go. I am fine. Come home with Sister."

Overcome by the shock of Baby talking to him, he quickly got back into the wagon and hurried home. He kept his eye on Netty, who huddled on the floor of the wagon, hiccupping quietly between her sobs. Pulling up to the barn, he hurriedly removed the harness from the horse and bedded her down. He hoped that would give Netty some extra time to compose herself, for she still seemed agitated. Returning to the wagon, he called to Netty.

When she didn't answer, he scooped her up and carried her to the stoop, expecting to find the door unlocked. But he could not get in. Rattling the door, he could feel the latch was still in place.

"How the devil are we going to get in now?" he muttered. "Baby must have climbed out of a window to follow us. Well, I guess I can just as easily go through a window to get in."

Leaning Netty against the wall, he turned to step off the stoop. He heard the rattle of the latch. Turning back to the door, he saw it open. And there stood Baby in all his golden glory.

Wil stood dumfounded. *How could Baby have gotten back before we did?* He'd have had to walk. And his goofy little wobble would take him days. *Wait a minute!* He could never have followed them to the church without help to begin with. He wouldn't have made it there on time.

Wil led Netty into the cabin, placing her on his bed near the fireplace. He quickly put on the tea kettle, taking comfort in its whistle as it came to a boil. Setting out two cups, he carried them over to Netty to cool. He saw Baby sitting next to her, softly stroking her tearstained face with his long fingers. Netty held tightly to Baby and buried her face in his fur.

"Netty, are we going to talk about this?"

"What is there to say, Wil?" Her voice sounded shaky. "You rescued me from a drunk and now we are home safe."

"No, Netty, you know that is not what I mean. I am sorry about the drunk. I guess we have been a little insulated here on the farm and forgot how judgmental other people can be about propriety."

"Wil, I am sorry if my unusual marital status caused you some embarrassment."

Glancing at Netty, he felt the stiffness in her tone. "Netty, you know that is not what I mean! How could I see Baby with you at the church and yet he arrived back here before we did?"

Netty sat silently looking down at her lap. Wil suddenly sat on the bed grabbing her shoulders. "*Look at me, Netty*. Look me in the eye. Now answer me. Can Baby fly?" He watched as she raised her head and looked into his eyes. Silent tears traveled slowly down her face.

"I love you, Wil, do you know that?" She said it so slowly, so sadly, that it gave Wil a chilling premonition. A now familiar pressure and golden aura whispered to him.

"Brother, I cannot fly. Sister cannot fly."

"I know Netty cannot fly, Baby, why would you mention that?" Wil asked the question, confused and distracted. No one spoke.

"*God damn it, Netty*, I need some answers here. What is going on? Are you hiding something from me? Why? You know I love you. Do you not trust me? I am going out of my mind trying to figure you out, but I do not think I can take much more." Wil dropped his hands and paced the floor. Baby had moved to the bedroom when Wil had started to get heated.

Slowly, Netty rose from Wil's bed. Her eyes were closed.

"Wil, could you come here, please? I would like one kiss right now, please." Wil stepped hesitantly over to Netty. He held her close and kissed her slowly. Netty felt all of his love and strength in that kiss. Her quiet bittersweet tears continued to fall.

"Netty, baby, please tell me what is happening."

Netty stepped back. She looked silently at Wil's beautiful, clear, dear face, trying to memorize every feature, dreading the outcome of the next critical moments. She closed her own eyes again and slowly unbuttoned her top. Slipping off her skirt, she took a painful breath. With a sob of anguish, she slipped off her petticoat. Standing in front of Wil with her head bowed in shame, her tail moved, circling around her waist protectively, reflecting its brilliance off the flame of the fire.

"*What the heck?* Netty, no." He backed up slowly, not taking his eyes off the shocking appendage. Netty sank to the bed, covering her nakedness with Wil's blanket. So much became clear to Wil.

"It was never about me was it, Netty?"

Netty shook her head, her voice a barely discernible croak. "No, Wil, I have always loved you."

"Netty, are you human?" Wil asked, knowing the pain that pierced Netty's heart with the question.

"I do not know what is happening to me, Wil. The changes started after I found Baby. I am scared. I do not know what it means," she admitted.

"What are we going to do?" Wil asked, sinking into a chair and dropping his face to his hands. He looked down at Netty. He could see the pain in her eyes as she turned her back, unable to face him any longer. Silence filled the room. Quietly, Wil confronted her.

"I still love you, Netty. And I love Baby. I just do not know if I can handle this. I need time to think. I am exhausted. I will sleep in the barn tonight." Grabbing his winter overcoat from a hook and an extra blanket kept at the foot of the bed, he walked out.

Netty knew crying herself to sleep would be fruitless. In the early hours of the morning she felt Baby, who had crept to her bed in the night, open the cabin door and slip out.

She woke late in the morning, the chill of the cabin a telltale sign that the fire had faded sometime in the night, just like her high hopes for herself and Wil. She felt empty, swollen and numb as she went to her bedroom to change into work skirt and apron. Baby was still missing. *He probably went with Wil to turn out the Jerseys.* She wondered where they were now. Had they gone to collect fieldstone as originally planned? Might Wil be planning to leave? She didn't think she could survive that. He was her love, her companion, her best friend. Could she go on living without him? Would she want to?

She nervously considered what she should do. She really wanted to climb back to bed, but the farm couldn't wait. Going out to the barn, she saw the wagon was missing. It appeared they'd turned out the Jerseys, then continued on with their chores. Lunchtime came and left. Why were they not back? Maybe Wil still wanted to be alone to think. Netty realized he must be starved. The night before, he'd hardly touched his dinner. She decided she should bring him some lunch and some cold well water, even though she hesitated to face him.

Walking slowly down the road to the field, she speculated on whether or not Wil could accept her after her revelation. Before Wil, her changes had turned her life into a nightmare, but she'd learned to live with them. Physically, it wasn't such a big deal. If the situation had happened in reverse, *she* could accept it. Couldn't she?

Netty looked up at the vibrant sun, noticing the unusual warmth for a late spring day. As she approached the field, she spotted the wagon with Maggie grazing nearby; Wil and Baby were nowhere in sight. She walked along the rock pile and spotted them both, further down the line. Wil was resting on the ground. It looked like he'd fallen asleep. Baby also appeared asleep, curled up next to him. As she moved closer, she noticed Baby seemed to be stroking Wil's hand. *What?* Breaking into a run, she screamed his name.

"*Willll!*"

Dropping to her knees, she held his face. Wil writhed in extreme pain, his breath labored and consciousness fading in and out. Looking up at the piles of fieldstone, she easily identified the deadly problem.

Quickly grabbing his arm, she dragged him away from the rock pile. Looking back, Netty spied a huge timber rattlesnake. Clambering over the rocks, she spotted numerous juvenile snakes. It looked like Wil had inadvertently discovered a nest of newborns. Their bites could be just as deadly as the adults'. They hadn't yet learned to conserve their venom for prey instead of a big dumb human looking for rocks.

"Baby, Wil is hurt. Why did you not call me?"

The pressure and rainbows whispered calmly, "Brother is dying."

"Dying? What do you mean, Baby? Wil cannot die, we need him." Netty screamed, raising her head to the sky, "Lord, my Father, *please help us.*" Looking down, she pleaded, "Make him better, Baby."

"It would be wrong. It is forbidden."

"Baby, you fixed me. Just do it again for Wil. Do you not love him?" Netty ran over to Baby in time to see him rise as a snake struck out and bit him. He slapped out at the snake, getting bitten again.

"Baby, g*et away from there!*" Netty ran toward Baby, then turned back as she heard Wil moan.

"*Oh my God*, someone, please help me," she screamed helplessly. Baby wobbled over to her, his arms outstretched, fingers working spastically. She snatched him up, looking for signs of the snake bites. Inexplicably, she found no signs of any wounds. She held him close, trying to calm him.

Setting him down again, she turned to Wil, wringing her hands. He could hardly breathe and ugly purple swellings were appearing all over his body. The venom was attacking his tissue. He would probably die.

Without thinking, Netty lifted her skirt, sat down and cradled his head. From somewhere far away came the feeling of pressure with the smell of sulfur. Netty looked up and saw her own tail in the air with a mature membrane receding inside. She felt light, fulfilled, complete. Silently, she raised her fearful eyes to Baby. *How did I do that?* Baby's slight head nodded. Netty understood. She looked at Wil and saw color returning to his face, his breathing normal again. Little by little, he began to focus.

"Netty, what are you doing here? *Snakes, watch out!*" Wil jumped up, looking for Baby. Snatching him up, he searched his tiny body for bites. "I saw you get bit, Baby, we need to get you to the doctor."

"No, Wil. Please sit down. You have been badly bitten."

"Netty, I am fine." Realizing the truth of what he'd just said, he sat down, bewildered. "Yes, I am fine." His voice faltered with astonishment. He looked at Baby. "Baby is fine, too. How can that be?"

"Wil, I do not know how to tell you this." Netty felt calm; the acceptance of her power inevitable. Wil stared.

"Did Baby do something or did you, Netty?" He gaped at her exposed tail.

"Wil, you were dying. Baby stayed by your side, but for some reason I do not understand, he is unable to heal you. Not just you but people in general."

"It was you, Netty? You healed me?" Wil's countenance reflected a broad canvas of conflicting emotions. "What does this mean?" Wil again looked at her tail. As he approached, he squatted down, haltingly touching the tail. It was warm and firm to the touch. If you set aside who the tail belonged to, it didn't look remarkable except for the bulbous tip and the amazing golden shine of the fine fur. Yes, fur on her tail. *Fur.* Just like Baby's. His brain refused to accept the impossible. His mind reeling, he flopped down in the dirt next to Netty. Holding her hands, he looked into her eyes. Her changes were impossible to ignore. The glow in her eyes pulsed deeper with a new intensity.

Pressure and brain auras flashing, the assailing whisper returned.

"Brother, you will be Elder. Together, we will be Elders. It is forbidden, but done is done. I shall ask the Womb to forgive. Sister didn't know, her control eluded her. We will wait for you to join us. Do not leave. I am pleased, Brother."

Baby shuffled over to Wil, bobbing all the way. He climbed up on to Wil's lap, stroking his face, his tapered leather fingers feathers of affection. Wil nuzzled Baby, wrapping his arms around him.

"It is all right, buddy, I am not going anywhere." Wil turned, assessing Netty's calm demeanor. "Can you please tell me what all this means before I go officially nuts?"

"I do not actually know that much, Wil. I know my appearance turns me into a freak, but I do not feel that way. I guess Baby means you will change now, just the way I have. I am pretty sure you will also develop a tail and have the same ability to heal. I am confused about why I should not have healed you. Baby tells me very little." Netty wrapped her arms around Wil. "Please, Wil, can we go back to the cabin and sort this out there?"

The three of them clung together, unaware of the large timber rattlesnake mother quietly slithering closer, her aggressive stance meant to protect her live newborn young.

As they rose awkwardly, Netty inadvertently stepped close to the aggressively coiled rattlesnake.

Startled out of her deeply emotional discourse by the sound of a warning rattle, Netty stumbled and fell, coming face to face with the snake. The protective mother instantly struck her in the face and again on her arm as her hands tried to fend it off. Wil picked up his nearby rifle and with a wicked thrust, brought the rifle down on the snake's head. The snake slithered quickly back toward the rocks, her head partially smashed and one eye crushed.

Immediately, they detected the heavy odor of sulfur as Baby and Netty both raised their tails, directing their life-saving power to the snake. Dumbfounded, they watched the snake freeze in place, shudder, then calmly continue to her nest in the rocks, a beautiful, vibrant, fully healed mature female.

Wil looked at Netty, now standing with her hands to her face. Slowly she lowered them, running her hands along her arm where she was bitten. Not a mark on her. Just like Baby.

Wil scooped up Baby without a word, Baby's head swiveling all the way around to watch the snakes. Wil took Netty by the hand and led them to Maggie and the wagon to take them back to the cabin.

They rode home in silence; the only sounds the clopping of Maggie's hooves and the reassuring rumble of the wagon's wheels on the rutted road. After stowing away Maggie and the wagon, they quietly returned to the cabin, tension now reigning. Baby curled up on Wil's bed by the fire, looking up at them alertly.

"Someone better start doing some explaining," demanded Wil, his voice incredulous. "And Baby, why were you going to let me die? I saw you heal the snake." Auras returned; the pressure lessening.

"Healing is an imperative. It is what Brothers and Sisters do. It is forbidden to create more Elders. I am forbidden to heal you."

"Who forbids it, Baby?"

"The Womb and the Elders."

"Where are the Elders, what the heck is a Womb and what are *you* exactly?"

"I am a proud minion of the Womb. The Elders expired eons ago, a devastating punishment for defying the Womb. No longer does the Womb grant immortality. Sister and I are now the only Elders. An honor and a privilege, although an error. You will soon join us. I am not unhappy about that. We will all be Elders together."

"Elders, what the heck does that even mean?" Wil slapped his leg in frustration. "Netty, are you an Elder like Baby says? Baby, where are you actually from?" The only answer they received was silence. Baby didn't speak again.

"I told you, Baby does not speak much. Wil, I know you are scared and upset, but this can all work out." Netty's pleading voice made his heart weep for her. "No one needs to know. This will be easier for you because you know what to expect. It took two years for my tail to grow. And I am fine. Apparently, better than fine." She touched her skin where it should have been broken by the bites.

"I do not want a tail, Netty. *I do not want this,*" Wil continued to rail, all thoughts of tenderness toward Netty gone. "I do not want this to be my life, do you understand?" Wil felt himself working his way up to a meltdown.

"Wil, please let us try to deal with this. We cannot change what has happened." Netty's low, calm voice was like warm syrup on Wil's frayed nerves. Slowly, he focused and calmed down. Standing to stretch, he paced the room, rubbing his palms together, relentlessly.

"Alright, Netty, alright." Wil sighed, sitting down. The cabin filled with silence, the only sound the crackle of the fire. Flames cast shadows on their strained faces, each waiting for the other to banish the silence.

"I love you, Wil."

He responded with unenthusiastic resignation. "I know you do, Netty, I love you, too."

Netty made a decision, the solution abundantly clear. Kneeling in front of him, she grasped his hand in hers. She slowly placed it on her breast as she engaged his eyes with hers, emotion and passion filling the space between them. She languidly skimmed her full lips across his. Wil groaned and whispered her name.

"Are you sure? Is it okay?"

"I have never been more positive about anything, for such a long, long time." Her face radiated her love and trust. "I was so afraid I would lose you if my secret were exposed. That is why I appeared to reject you. I felt ashamed. We can solve our other problems tomorrow. Tonight, I want us to be together," Netty whispered, the unrestrained passion clear in her voice. "Trust me, it will make everything easier."

Wil swept her up in his arms, his lips seeking hers. Fire exploded between them, breathless groans filled the room. Rising, they broke apart to bashfully beam at one another. Hope back in her heart, quixotic as life itself, Netty led Wil to her bedroom. With a quick wave to Baby, she delightedly shut the door and opened her mind to the possibility of a brand new life.

Wil and Netty woke very early the next morning. Netty stayed in bed while Wil rounded up Baby and went to turn out the Jerseys. They immediately returned to the bedroom where Netty waited. Wil jumped back into bed and together they watched Baby shuffle and bob over to the bed, clambering up to squeeze himself in between them. They burst out laughing, hugging Baby and smiling into each other's eyes as they sparkled with life, the new easy intimacy of lovers a boon to their morning.

Wil and Netty's life settled back down to the hard work they espoused. With Netty's newly found confidence, she discovered new strength and tolerance toward her body. Wil gracefully accepted the inevitability of his changes with her guidance. Now, when their customers shopped at the vegetable stand, or accepted delivered produce, their new status tolled their love, loud as a church bell. Most were very happy for them, even as a few still sniffed at their sinful behavior.

Wil eventually managed to hire two new field hands to help him with the planting. The new hands joined them in the fields for picking, as Netty's miracle seed continued to out-produce anything seen before. Extra time to devote to the baking and churning came easily, and their sizable increase in profits escalated the plan for the new bakery. Netty obsessively finished her work at night in time to join Wil in bed, often swatting Baby back to the kitchen. No matter what they did, though, Baby always found his way back to bed, wedged firmly between them. They agreed it was just too darn hard to say no to the lovable creature.

Fall descended on the farm like a grande dame preparing to replace her luxurious wardrobe for next season's fashions. Wil was busy hiring Italian laborers who worked long hard hours to complete the bakery. With the completion of the foundation and walls, the two huge fieldstone ovens in the middle of the floor began to take shape. The space allowed Netty to cook a dozen pies at a time. Interior wood boxes allowed firewood to stay dry all winter. Wil's design enabled Netty to better organize her utensils for maximum efficiency. They even discussed the merits of taking on an apprentice to help her in the bakery.

Miracle of miracles, on the day of Netty's twenty fifth birthday, they discovered they were going to have a baby. Most would say pregnancy is unseemly unless you were married to the father. But Wil and Netty refused to accept conventional wisdom. Their jubilance merely gilded their perfect life. The more the bakery grew, the more Netty grew. She realized the time to look into her divorce had long passed. As much as she didn't want their child to grow up a bastard, she wanted more than anything to be Mrs. Wil Capaccino.

Time continued to pass in a haze of laughter, hard work and love. A now seven months pregnant Netty necessarily slowed down. Her pregnancy began to show inevitable signs of difficulty. The constant vomiting worried her: she thought it should have stopped by now. She never felt like eating so she didn't know how she even had anything to vomit up. She also developed a curious desire to lie in the sun, feeling it seep deep into her body and leaving her feeling enriched and less nauseous.

Wil and Baby were doing their best to cover for her. Wil helped with the pies and Baby made a stab at the churn. That was quite a sight. They found Baby never stopped giving them something to laugh about. They idly wondered how Baby would take to their impending bundle of joy, hoping he would celebrate along with them. After all, he was nothing if not joyful about new life.

Netty prepared to make a delivery to a neighbor about two miles down the road. She knew Farmer Neal from her schoolhouse when she was a child. His young wife was also pregnant. Netty wanted to make this delivery herself so she could spend some time with the farmer's wife and compare pregnancies. She promised Wil this would be her last delivery over the bumpy roads.

The lovely March day beckoned, a promise of spring growth around the corner in time to celebrate the end of the construction of the bakery. It had taken every penny of their savings. Netty found herself busy making clothes and diapers for the baby, who would arrive in less than two months. They'd just finished converting the little addition Wil had put on the kitchen during his first year at the farm into a space for the baby's crib. Wil had built the crib, of course, his excitement refused to be corralled.

Netty's thoughts darkened as she remembered Wil complaining of an ache at the very small of his back. He hadn't yet realized what it meant. With the joy of the baby's arrival, she continually pushed away all thoughts of his impending tail. She hoped Wil would be better able to handle his change with the distraction of the baby. Oh well, she knew they would handle *anything* life threw at them. They were an unbeatable resilient team. How many more difficulties could God possibly throw their way?

Netty pulled up to the Neal farm after lunch, tying the wagon to the old hitch, the Neal's shiny new Ford truck parked in front of their well-maintained barn. She didn't plan to be more than an hour or so.

Knocking on the door, Mrs. Neal answered, inviting her in for tea and happily relieving her of her basket of fresh fruit. She sat in the elaborate kitchen of the Neal's spacious home, quite luxurious by her own standards.

Farmer Neal had a huge herd of Jerseys with vast pastures, confided Ruthann, his wife, still eyeing the unbelievable size of the fruit in Netty's gift basket. Obviously, they too worked hard for their prosperity.

Ruthann rattled on about the farm and their plans for the newborn. They enjoyed their tea and each other's company as the hour passed.

As Netty rose to take her leave, she asked Ruthann if she might first use the privy. Laughing, Ruthann showed her the way out the back door. Netty knew she'd never have made it home without relieving herself; the baby was pressed uncomfortably against her bladder. Her stomach felt like a dead weight as the baby kicked her sharply.

Upon finishing her toilet, Netty returned to the house, letting herself in through the back door. She paused as she heard voices in the kitchen: men's voices. She could hear them discussing business.

Netty hesitated to interrupt and turned to let herself back out when she heard Robert's name mentioned.

Now listening closely, she could make out something about raising the rent on the farm. She heard Mr. Neal object, saying Mr. Woods had never raised his rent this often. The other voice also sounded familiar.

Peeking around the corner, she saw none other than Eli, her husband's man. He flailed his arms at Farmer Neal, insisting that the land belonged to Robert Doyle; the Neal family had little choice since they didn't own the land.

Netty pressed herself tightly to the wall, hoping not to be seen. Her heart raced as she slowly backed out the door and ran around the house to the wagon. Clumsily, she pulled herself up as the front door opened and Eli appeared.

She backed the wagon away from the hitching post, hurrying away. Giving a quick glance back, she saw Eli standing there, just looking after her. *Has he recognized me? Will the Neals say anything? Will Eli ask?*

This was a bad omen. Not having to deal with Robert had allowed her the freedom to create a new life. This timing called an end to her good luck and peace of mind; but the Neals' farm? They pay rent to Robert? Were there others? Actually, how big *was* two thousand acres?

Rushing back to the farm, she found Wil at the bakery, painting it, while Baby played in the barn. Quickly, she related the news to Wil.

"You said two thousand acres? Netty, are you kidding me? I doubt the whole town is even one thousand acres. Netty, you are really rich. And that bastard of a husband is cheating you. He has obviously been collecting the rents from the lease-holders and the tenement farmers for years. We need to hire a lawyer as soon as we can to get him out of your life. He is stealing from you."

"You do not know him, Wil, he is ruthless. He raped and murdered my mama. I do not think it will be that easy."

"Do not worry, babe." Wil rubbed her tummy and gave her a quick kiss on the lips. "You have me now. And we have big ol' Baby for backup." He laughed as they spied Baby shuffling and wobbling toward them from the barn. Baby held something in his arms. A barn kitten. He'd discovered the mama cat giving birth five weeks ago and had made himself their protector. He proudly showed them off whenever Wil or Netty would pay attention. They each took a turn to admire the kitten. Baby shuffled off, heading back to the barn.

"Netty, why don't I saddle Maggie and run into town? I can sit down with a lawyer and see where you stand legally."

"Yes, that might be a good idea," Netty considered carefully. "We need to get information right now. I am going to work on some pies in the kitchen then start dinner. Try to hurry home." Netty kissed him goodbye and Wil hurried after Baby to the barn.

Netty finished the last of the pies. Sliding them into the oven to bake, she began peeling a four-pound potato for dinner. She heard the latch on the front door. Calling to Baby, she turned, her mouth freezing in mid-sentence. There stood Eli.

"How *dare* you come into my home? What do you want?" Her voice ricocheted indignantly.

"Well, well, Miz Doyle." He leaned lazily against the back of the door, insolence defining his posture. "Sounds like yer not all that happy ta see me. Thought I would stop by before I head back to Norristown ta see how yer doin'." Eli sauntered further into the room, his bulk blocking the door, cutting off her escape.

"I am sure the boss is gunna be happy to hear how well yer doin' here, means he can sure get a better price for the land when he sells it to that fancy group from New York City."

Netty attempted to prevent her shock registering on her face. Any weakness simply inflamed bullies.

Eli inched closer. "Don't know how he's gunna feel with you carryin' that drifter's bastard, though. Nah, he's not gunna like hearin' that a'tol." Eli reached out, grabbing her elbow, and pulled her so close she could smell the stench of his breath.

"Thought I'd not recognize ya, gal? Ya sure look holier than thou with all that gold hair now, don' cha?" He grabbed her pony tail, giving it a twist. He wrapped it around her throat, flipping her around, then came up behind her. She could feel his erection throbbing against her back.

"Please, Eli, my baby," she whispered.

Eli dragged her over to the old straw bed and threw her down. She landed with a wince on her stomach. She could see him actually slobbering as he leered over her.

"Never wanted ta take a piece of ya when the boss said I could, but I sure think I'll help myself to a piece right now." Flipping her over on her back, he pulled down his pants. Netty tried to kick him, but he grabbed her leg, letting loose with a backhand across her face. Strangely, she felt no pain. But the baby felt different. Something must be wrong. She had to protect the baby.

"My baby, something is wrong. You need to go." She tried to get up, causing Eli to use his foot on her stomach, shoving her back on the straw bed. She felt something pull loose in her womb. Shaking uncontrollably, she tried to shield her abdomen.

"*God no*, please. My baby."

"Oh, ya gonna be nice, now? Thought ya might change yer mind when ya saw what a real man looked like. Let me hear ya say ya want it, Netty gal. Come on, let me hear it." Eli raised his fist.

"Just get it over with, please." Her voice was reduced to a whimper, and she tried to blank out her mind as Eli raped her. She could get through this. The baby would be fine, Eli would leave. She still had Wil and Baby. *Baby. Oh my gosh; where is Baby? Baby, stay in the barn, please,* she prayed silently.

Eli's weight on top of her felt oppressive. She felt her stomach being compressed as he assaulted her in her most tender and private area. Her tail, wadded up under her waist, cramped from the painful crushing. As Eli finished, she felt blood pool between her legs.

"Oh no, oh no," she moaned. Rolling off the bed, she tried to stand. Her legs buckled and down she went. Holding her stomach, she screamed at Eli. "I need a doctor, please help me."

"Git that wop drifter a yur's ta help. I gotta git back ta Norristown ta give the boss his rents. Ya weren't worth da effort anyway. Ya better keep your trap shut now, hear?" Looking at the blood pooled around her, he sneered.

"What the heck?" Sniffing, he detecting the odor of sulfur that leached from her blood; blood that glimmered, not just red but distinct tones of effervescence. "Looks like ya got yourself a real problem, for Christ's sake, gal." Grimacing, he let himself out the door.

Netty touched the liquid pooling around her. It was very warm, and she could feel heat radiate from it. When she put her fingers in it, the blood parted, leaving her hand dry. *What?* She gathered her skirt, pressing into her groin to stop the flow. She felt something hitch inside her. She tried to remember when she'd last felt the baby move. It had to have been when Wil had left for town. She considered the color of her blood as she felt a slow dawning of terror, her pulse racing dangerously. *What does it mean? Is this another of my changes? How will it affect the baby? Will the baby be normal?* Her head was spinning. She had to calm down. *Wil, where are you? Please, come home.*

Netty rocked and held her skirt closely as she felt contractions. The baby was coming. *No, it is too early, God please, I beg you.* Tears silently streamed from twin pools of desperate anguish. Slowly, she pulled herself over to the bed to lie down. Just in time, as she felt another gush between her legs. Netty's eyes rolled back in her head and she mercifully passed out.

Wil unhitched the wagon, leading the horse to his stall. Filling the water trough, he thought he should bring the Jerseys down from the pasture before he went in for dinner. That would enable him to linger with Netty before he did the milking. Rounding up Baby from his kitten protection detail in the hay loft, he saddled up Maggie and together they started out for the cow pasture trail. As Wil rounded up the Jerseys with Baby holding the gate open, he thought of the information supplied by the lawyer. It appeared they had a tough row to hoe. Even if they could prove their case of fraud, Robert Doyle now wielded a great deal of influence. He was the Norris County magistrate. That position entitled him to privileges in Sussex County where the subject property was. The rumor mill also suggested Robert *owned* many men in law enforcement, with those in town on his payroll as they engaged in distributing the bootleg rum made in his carriage house at Sunnydale.

Wil was not yet deterred. He really needed to discuss things with Netty first and planned to broach the subject after dinner. He didn't want her to stress until after she ate. He rarely saw her put food in her mouth anymore. *Well, at least she has not been losing weight.*

Arriving at the barn, Baby slipped down from Maggie, dashing toward the hayloft. After giving Maggie a quick brush down and some oats, he collected Baby, pausing to admire the kittens at Baby's insistence. Scooping Baby up and swinging him up on his shoulders, he left the barn.

Mounting the stoop, he noticed the cabin door was ajar.

Not a good idea, Wil thought. *I will have to speak to Netty about that.* Entering the cabin, he choked. The room was filled with smoke, the smell of burnt fruit pies and sulfur. Shooing Baby back out the door, he shouted for Netty. Running to the ovens, he opened the doors and pulled out the ruined pastries. Hearing a moan from the straw bed, he spied Netty lying there. A glowing liquid seemed to be spread over the floor and down Netty's legs. Her tail, with its ominous membrane, hovered helplessly over her head. In Netty's arms lay what was left of their baby.

"I could not heal the baby," Netty said in a tiny tin voice. She sounded empty and lost, clearly in shock.

Tears slipped down Wil's face as he quickly ran to her side. Slipping to his knees, he put his hands on her head, smoothing back her damp hair. Her eyes were open but unfocused. She clung to their infant who was clearly dead, its skin blue underneath a sickly sheen of what appeared to be an effervescent membrane.

Netty focused on Wil and seemed to recognize him. Pitifully, she cried. "He raped me, Wil," she whispered. "He hurt the baby. He hurt our baby."

"Who was here, Netty? Who did this to you?" Wil's face

tightened bitterly, his guts contracting. He felt as though he could not breathe.

"It was Eli. He recognized me. It was my fault. I should have stayed home." Netty curled up around her dead child, murmuring to it. Slowly, she sat up, her eyes feverish.

"Baby, where is he? *He can save the baby*. He can bring him back." Scooting to the edge of the bed, she staggered to her feet, weaving to the door and calling for Baby. She fell to the floor as she lost her footing, Wil running to her side. The door opened to Baby sitting on the stoop where Wil had left him. Netty held the infant in her arms, offering her dead child to the creature.

"You can do it, Baby, I have tried, but nothing happened. But you can do it, Baby, you know how." Netty dissolved into incoherent tears as Baby just stared, unmoving. Wil tried to drag her back into the cabin, but she resisted. "Baby, please. *You have to help me*," she shouted hysterically. Turning to Wil, she begged, "Please get Baby to help me. He will listen to you."

Colorful auras flashed, iridescence mixed with pressure. The whispers tried to calm her. "Sister, I cannot. The life is already gone."

Netty sat on the floor, limp and stunned. Wil gently eased the stillborn from her arms, holding it tenderly to his chest. He wiped away his silent tears as he wrapped their baby in a blanket and took it to the barn. He would bury his child later, after attending to Netty.

Returning to the cabin, he found Netty still on the floor by the door with Baby at her side, stroking her face. He poured Netty a cup of water, but she pushed it away. Forcing her up, he carried her into their bedroom. He peeled off her damp filthy clothes before pulling a clean nightgown over her head. Slipping her under the covers, he lay down next to her, cradling her in his arms until she drifted off to sleep. The last words she said were, "He hurt the baby."

Wil sat at the table in the kitchen while Netty slept. His pain and anger percolated hotly, quickly heading to a boil. His teeth clenched so hard he could feel his facial muscles spasm. Not a man prone to violence, he contemplated only one course of action. He needed an eye for an eye. Reluctant to rely on the legal system with the threat of Robert Doyle's influence, he resolved to handle the matter himself.

Carefully, he wrote a note for Netty. He carried it into her bedroom where Baby was watching her. He kissed her head, setting the note on her nightstand.

"Baby, lock the door behind me. I will be back in four days. I will send one of the field hands to take care of the Jerseys. Stay in the house until I am back. Netty needs you now." Patting Baby on the head he left the bedroom, stalking out of the cabin with one of their rifles.

Chapter 6

Robert sat in his library, elegantly sipping from a hand-blown crystal snifter. He enjoyed watching the color of his favorite brandy, looking through the glass as he rotated the crystal in the light of the fire. Eli was overdue, but he should arrive momentarily. He'd better. Anticipation made him restless. He anxiously awaited the pleasure he derived from tabulating the income Eli had collected from Netty's tenement farmers. He smiled to himself, thinking of the windfall the land was bringing him, even though he'd lost the other deal on the acreage shortly after Netty ran off.

He thought about Netty. He rarely worried about her. He knew how to find her. Where *else* would she be likely to go? He'd heard the rumors of the drifter she'd allowed to take up residence with her. Together they'd apparently made quite an improvement to the property. Maybe he wouldn't sell it just yet, after all. He didn't fear Netty or her drifter. *Well, well, she has turned out to be a wanton trollop after all, has she not?* He chuckled to himself, thinking of the rumored age difference between the two. He dismissed the strange tales of Netty's produce and her orchards, along with the gossip about Netty's looks. How the cow had even been able to attract the drifter was beyond him. He thought seriously about killing them both. He could make it look as if the drifter had done it. Then he would go in as the patient and forgiving husband, deftly claiming the property.

The sale of some of the acreage would make things much easier for him. His sisters had developed a habit of stopping by to complain about their shortness of funds, expecting him to subsidize them after their wealthy husbands put them on leashes. Their expenses overwhelmed him. He thought of the horses, their yearly wardrobes, their entertaining and the extravagant galas, all pathetic attempts to stay relevant. Their husbands had long ago exhausted their patience with their spending, but Robert found it difficult to say no. Perhaps it was because, as their only brother, he felt a familial obligation. Or maybe, as the youngest, he found it the only way to lord over them. Either way, they created a significant drain on his finances.

A more pressing concern involved a rumor he'd heard at the courthouse. Only a whisper as of yet, but it appeared the federal government was weighing the benefits of legalizing alcohol, *actually repealing Prohibition*. That would be disastrous for him. If true, he might not have much time, although the feds were notoriously inept.

Taking another sip, his housekeeper appeared. Big Martha's name fit her precisely. She was big and black, her impassive face clearly having seen plenty, wisely knowing how to keep all to herself.

"Mr. Eli done returned, Mr. Doyle, sir. He sent word up from the carriage house. Sure, sure. He says ta tell you he gone an picked up a present for you from one a the farms he visited. He said she be needin' some supper. I kin fix them sum'un or would you be wantin' ta see him right away?"

"Feed the young lady, Martha; then send her up to my bedroom. Give her one of the usual garments to change into. The blue, I think tonight. I trust it has been properly repaired since last time? And tell Eli to get in here, now."

"Yesum, sir. Sure, sure." As Big Martha left, bobbing her head, Eli popped up behind her, sporting a big grin. He set the money bag down on Robert's desk and pulled up a chair. Without asking, he helped himself to some of Robert's brandy, gulping it down.

"Easy there, bucko, that is mighty expensive stuff," Robert said, clearly annoyed.

"Relax, boss, I deserve it after the ride I gave ol' Netty." Robert favored Eli with a raised eyebrow. "Yeah, I ran inta her by accident. Did ya know she got knocked up? I had a lucky chance ta show her what a real man looked like, so I took it. I did leave her a wee bit worse for the wear. I think the bastard babe might not a made it."

"Well, you may have saved me some trouble. But let me know next time before you decide to do something like that," Robert said, mildly irked. "Did you see any sign of the wop she's shacked up with? What kind of shape did you leave her in?"

"She was in pretty bad shape. All this weird shit coming out of her, thought it was blood, but I don' think so. She was holler'n for a doctor when I left." He chuckled. "Sump'n bout the kid."

"Well, dummy, you may have created a little problem for us if he shows up here. If she can identify you, I bet he will. You should have just twisted her ugly neck on the way out, Eli. Clean up your mess like a man."

"She's not an ugly twit anymore, boss. If the farmer I was collectin' from din' tell me who she was I wouldn't a known. I knew I had ta have a piece a that." Casting his eyes down, he belatedly remarked, "Hope you don't mind, boss."

"No, but we better be ready if he shows up." Looking at how the fire glinted off his gold coin collection (*minus one coin, the bitch, I know she took it*), he gathered inspiration, hatching a beautiful plan. Yes, quite perfect. It would easily remove one annoying obstacle from his road to the fair Netty and solve Eli's problem at the same time.

"Eli, it is time for me to have my evening entertainment. Thank you, by the way. If any spirit remains after I am finished, I will send her to your room. If not, I will ring as usual and you can dispose of her. Please remember to remove the gown first. Drop it off with the housekeeper for repairs in the morning. I am sure it still has some wear left in it. If Netty's drifter shows up, wake me, regardless of the time."

Robert stood, bidding goodnight to Eli. He moved to his safe where he deposited the receipts from Eli's last collection. Passing the prominent display of his coin collection, he paused. With a devilish grin, he removed two of the coins, slipping them into the pocket of his opulent dressing gown. He gave a satisfied shake of his head and mounted the stairs to his bedroom, relishing the anticipation of the evening's pleasures.

The long journey to Norristown wore Wil down, yet his vengeance still simmered ominously. Maggie plodded with fatigue, holding up like a champ. He knew he couldn't be that far behind the bastard that had torn apart his life. Poor Netty, she didn't deserve any of this. He tried not to cry as he thought about what the loss of their baby might do to them. Pushing the thoughts from his head, he tried to concentrate on a plan. He felt sure he could find Sunnydale without much trouble. After all, how many hulking mansions did one city have?

Before long, he managed to locate the Doyle estate. Predictably, it was located on the best street in the city. He tied Maggie to a tree down the block. If anything went wrong he didn't want her involved. He knew someone would find and care for her until the time came to reclaim her. For added insurance, he wrote down his name and address, tucking it inside his saddlebag.

Creeping on to the property, he watched the front door without seeing any activity. The luminous moon beamed prominently, exposing the manicured lawn along with Wil's inadequate hiding place. He silently reconnoitered the estate, sneaking around the side of the house to watch the back door. Still no activity.

He shook the weariness from his tired swollen eyes as he wondered what it had been like for Netty to live in this huge mansion. *How am I going to quickly find Eli on this property? And what will I actually do when I find him? Can I shoot him?* He realized no jury would find him sympathetic if he shot a man in cold blood, even if the man had raped his woman and caused the death of his unborn baby. He felt the rush of blood in his ears as he imagined his callused hands around Eli's neck. Maybe it would be better if he shot them both, Robert *and* Eli.

He stared at the back door, wondering how many people were inside the house. He needed to simmer down and plan this carefully.

Through the trees at the back of the property he observed flickers of light. It must be the carriage house where Robert conducted his bootleg business. *How many people does he employ? Will they come running if they hear a gunshot?* Wil's mind swirled with options and terror. He'd be worthless to Netty in jail, leaving her even more vulnerable and damaged. He shifted his body, feeling cramped and uncomfortable. Desperation to get back to Netty further frayed his reserves. Before long, Wil's eyes drooped, allowing deadly sleep to claim him, mercifully allowing his demons a respite.

Startled awake by the sound of a far off gun shot, his heart thudded rapidly, causing him to break into an acrid sweat. Widening his eyes, he saw the barrel of his own rifle sighting down at him. *What the—?*

Strong arms grabbed him, lifting him off his feet. He felt a solid punch to his solar plexus, squashing his breath back down his trachea. Another fist mainlined right to his face. They dropped him to the ground, stomping him thoroughly. A boot landed in his face, smashing his nose, another kicked at his kidneys. The men suddenly stopped as a large man in a dressing gown approached. He held one hand in his pocket. Ordering the men to pick Wil up, he put one arm around his shoulders, prompting him to stumble to the front of the house.

Blood dripped from Wil's nose briefly, then stopped. He straightened up, the pain from his beating gone as suddenly as if whisked away. Grateful, he remembered Netty and Baby's rapidly healed snake bites. Slapping him on the back, the big man gave Wil a long glacial glare.

"Well, you sure took that beating well." He searched Wil's body looking for signs of injury from the brutal thrashing inflicted on him. The man's eyes narrowed. "Go home, boy. Before I have my boys give you another dose of our hospitality."

Wil slowly walked down the drive, now minus his rifle, disconsolate and wondering why he'd wasted time on this futility. His confusion distracted him so much, he failed to sense the weight of two gold coins, now nestled comfortably in the back pocket of his work pants. He trudged down the road to collect Maggie, defeat and humiliation weighing him down like a child who'd just lost his underwear to a schoolyard bully. He should never have come. He should have stayed with Netty. She needed him more than he needed to vent his anger. He felt awash in impotence and faced a very long ride home.

Poor Maggie, she was in for a long haul again, too. At least she'd been able to rest. Maybe he could locate some oats and water for her before they took off. Rounding the bend where he'd left her tied up, he spotted her lying on the ground, her face splattered in blood. *What the—?* Running up to her, his shocked eyes tried to deny the truth of the fresh bullet hole in her temple, brain splatter creeping from underneath her velvet majestic head. *No. Not Maggie, please—not my beautiful girl.* He slumped his head down on hers. She still felt warm, but he knew: She was gone. *Oh, God, why? What have I done to displease you so?* Overcome with shock, he kissed her still damp tender muzzle, lay down in the dirt and broke down, thoroughly defeated.

Chapter 7

Netty frequently lost track of time, but thought it had been at least two weeks since Wil had left the cabin, forcing her to wonder if she might lose her sanity if he stayed away one more day.

"You are sure he said four days, Baby?"

"Yes, Sister; four rotations of the sun happened many rotations ago. I do not think Brother is coming back."

"Why do you say that, Baby? Wil would *never* desert us. We are a family. He loves us. He knows we are waiting for him."

"I know, Sister. I need Brother to bring Maggie back. It is time to turn out the Jerseys. Maybe I need to go and find him." The aura faded from her mind as Baby's long fingers closed spasmodically, a sure sign of agitation. She pulled Baby up to her lap for comfort, her endless tears dripping down to soak into his fur as she reflected on their lonely wait.

She'd woken the day after she lost the baby, feeling like a hunk of dead meat that didn't know enough to stay down. Baby clung, thankfully, to her side every moment. She'd forced herself up to check on the Jerseys and found Wil's note. Reading, she realized Wil had gone to find Eli. A better solution might have been to call the sheriff, if only they owned a telephone. She needed Wil desperately. She just wanted his arms around her, telling her things would be good again. She'd walked around the cabin in a time warp, not bathing, dressing or combing her now ratty hair. What was the point without Wil?

She'd been forced to bury their child by herself. She'd found it wrapped up in the barn where Wil had set the poor thing. At least Baby had accompanied her while she said goodbye. They did it together. Throwing dirt on her and Wil's baby as it lay in the primitive grave felt like throwing dirt on their past life together.

She'd held Baby tightly as she cried over the grave, rocking him slowly in her arms. They'd walked back to the cabin and slept long hours. She'd known the Jerseys were being tended to by Wil's helpers. Luckily, she found she'd suffered no lasting damage from the assault. She refused to use the word rape. Denial was her current means of exerting control in a world that left her feeling like flotsam at the mercy of a hurricane. So she just slept while she waited for Wil to come home.

Almost three weeks had passed by the time she seriously considered searching for him. She was in the kitchen when she heard a knock and, shooing Baby into the bedroom, she answered the door. It was Farmer Neal from down the road.

"Howdy, Netty," he said, removing his hat. He danced from side to side as if he had to urinate. "Well now, ah oh, shoot. You sure have been good to my Ruthann, so I thought I should be the one to tell you. We were in town last week and we heard tell that Wil was in jail. They said he got arrested for stealing. Got him dead to rights down the road from where it happened. They say he shot his horse and tried to blame it on someone else. Sorry to give you the news, Netty." Looking down, he noticed she was no longer pregnant. "Well, well, Netty, looks like the baby came. Congratulations. Be seeing you now." And with a tip of his hat, he disappeared off the stoop.

Netty stood motionless, her brain stunned, then overcome with panic. She heated some water on the fireplace and washed in her bedroom. Her hair was a mess. She pulled it back quickly. Running to the barn, she got their other horse and hooked up the wagon. She instructed Baby to lock the door and not come out for anything.

Quickly, she rode toward town. Maggie shot by Wil? Never. *Absolutely not.* Maybe Farmer Neal had got the story wrong. She knew for sure that Wil hadn't stolen a darn thing. Choking back a sob, she urged the horse to hurry. She arrived in town just after lunch, making a beeline for the sheriff's office.

Entering one of the only brick buildings, she felt her anxieties return, wondering what she needed to say. Should she report Wil as missing? Should she report Farmer Neal's story? Should she report the rape? She decided she must first find Wil.

Walking up to the desk at the front of a large reception room, she asked for the sheriff. Explaining he was in a meeting, the receptionist suggested she could wait if she liked. Netty decided she would. She took a seat furthest from the front door. It offered some measure of privacy, sheltered behind a wall that projected partially into the room. The small wall displayed all kinds of official bulletins. Netty hoped they might be revealing.

Time passed slowly as Netty read the bulletins. Townspeople bustled in and out on various errands. Many found time just to shoot the breeze and pass the time with the sheriff's receptionist.

As Netty scanned the sheriff's bulletins, she noticed Mr. Simpson, the creepy butcher, enter with a deputy. Just then, the sheriff came into the room and joined them. For some reason, Netty thought to shrink tight against the wall where she couldn't be seen. She was just close enough to see Mr. Simpson clap the sheriff on the arm. Not wanting to eavesdrop, she looked out the window. She snapped her attention back to the room when she heard Mr. Simpson whisper coarsely.

"Hear you found an easy way to part that upstart drifter, Wil Capaccino from Netty Doyle's property. Does the boss have any plans to get rid of him for good or is he just gunna go for the land now that she's easy pickings?"

"We need to take things slow. I think Doyle is going to let him rot in jail until he comes up with a plan to grab the property. These things are getting harder and harder to cover. His men, that includes you, Simpson, tend to get a little too bloodthirsty for me. Go easy on her, won't you? I do not want an unexplainable body to dispose of. I would like to avoid raising a lot of uncomfortable questions."

The sheriff shook hands with Mr. Simpson and escorted him to the door. Turning, he spotted Netty sitting against the wall. His face froze. Shaking off his surprise, he approached her.

"Well, Mrs. Doyle, is there some way I can help you today?"

Netty had heard enough to realize what she was up against. Robert must have quite a few in this town on his payroll. The best thing to do was to act as if she'd heard nothing. But she still needed information. She swallowed quickly to steady her voice.

"I understand Wil is in jail. Can you tell me what he is accused of and where he might be?"

"Well, Mrs. Doyle, he is accused of stealing some valuable gold coins from your husband in Norristown. He was thrown in jail after court by Mr. Doyle himself. He *is* the chief magistrate now, you know."

"So, he is in jail in Norristown? When will he be getting out?"

"Don't know that he will be getting out. Seems he shot one of Mr. Doyle's horses. Tried to claim the horse as his own, but then could not explain why he had shot it. He had some dandy story that Doyle's men shot the horse and framed him. Mr. Doyle had a lot of witnesses. You know what happens to a horse thief. Sorry I cannot help you, Mrs. Doyle, but they will probably hang him in time. Good day." Tipping his hat to Netty he returned to his office, leaving her standing frozen to the spot, her face a bloodless mask.

The sheriff watched Netty rush out the door and run down the street. Calling his deputy, he quickly wrote a letter and sealed it. The telephone party line needed to be avoided with a matter as sensitive as this.

"Deliver this to the boss. He better know she may be up to something, might need to step up his plans. She could start some trouble for us if we are not careful."

Netty ran blindly down the street. She felt totally alone. Who could she trust in this town? She now realized she and Wil had kept to themselves far too much. She had no friends to turn to, only Baby and Wil. They were all she'd ever needed. Even her customers weren't to be trusted. There was no way of knowing what name sat on Robert's payroll, plotting against her to steal her land. But she must still save Wil.

Wringing her hands, she frantically scanned the sparsely crowded street, recognizing no one. She needed someone connected to the court system. She must avoid anyone with clout or success, in case they were loyal to Robert. She just needed a lead on how to proceed.

Rounding a corner, she spotted a pathway that led to the poorly frequented part of town. Rotted garbage lay along a few boarded up store fronts, a door with screechy hinges banged loudly. As she considered the wisdom of her presence there, an unseen child screamed at an imagined insult, the sound echoing down the street.

This was the black section of town. Most towns didn't even let them own property, but this town fostered a huge respect for a man's hard work, and many hardworking blacks had found a home here. Netty stumbled down the pathway to the only building that showed any sign of life. She heard southern hill music coming from inside the dark building. Stepping up to the open door, she entered. She peered through the dimness, smelling heavily sweating, musky male bodies and something she suspected was spirits.

As her eyes adjusted to the gloom, she noticed every black face turned her way. She hesitated as the room stopped all motion, a sudden silence drawing further eyes her way. Silence ticked loudly.

"You aut not ta be here, M'sus." She heard a deep voice emanate from the gloom.

"Gentlemen, ah, if you could just give me a moment of your time? I am sorely in need of advice." Her faltering words were met with unfriendly stares. "Please, I mean no one any harm. I am looking for your legal adviser; if you could just direct me." Her pleading voice petered out. Netty couldn't hold back tears as she realized this was a dead end.

Turning, she made her way back to the door when she heard a voice say, "Reverend Penny, Misus. You best be leav'in now, b'for there be trouble. Pretty lady like you don' belong here." Nodding her thanks, Netty backed out of the little building, tripping over her feet on the way out.

Retracing her steps, she made it back to the main thoroughfare.

Finding her way to her wagon, she drove to the square where the churches clustered. She was looking for the Baptist Church, the only church that would accept the small number of black families from the area. Reverend Penny was rumored to not see black or white, only God's children. She should have thought of him to begin with. Netty approached the church, admiring the beauty of its stunning stained glass windows; very expensive stained glass. The congregation must be larger than she realized. Entering the church, she looked down to the altar where Reverend Penny and a little black child stood together.

The tearful girl of about six years held a small dog in her arms that looked crushed, probably by the wheel of a wagon or the tire of one of the new automobiles in town. Its rear leg lay at an unnatural angle, a grisly bone exposed. It hung limply in the child's arms as her tears fell on its face, causing the dog to whine pitifully. She overheard the child ask Reverend Penny if God could please heal her doggie.

Netty's tail, lying comfortably hidden under her skirt, suddenly unwound, rising into the air. She tried franticly to rein the unbridled appendage in, appalled by her inconceivable lack of control.

The church quickly filled with the smell of sulfur. Her tail soared as the membrane shot out its healing pressure, directed at the puppy. As the dog wiggled out of the child's arms, Netty quickly sat down in a pew, hoping to be overlooked.

The child ran up the aisle, calling to her dog as it emerged from the church, ready to resume battle with wagon wheels. Reverend Penny, flummoxed by the pup's startling transformation, collapsed on the floor.

Hurrying to the altar, her tail now firmly tucked under her skirt, she rushed to the reverend, helping him to his feet. He appeared dazed, confusion obscuring his pious carriage. Introducing herself without pause, Netty requested a private word.

"My dear, did you see a young child with a dog run outside?"

"Yes, Reverend, I did."

"The dog, he was running on all four legs?"

"Yes, Reverend, he was."

Reverend Penny slowly turned to the golden cross on the altar and on bent knee, genuflected. Netty mulled over what had just happened. She knew the more she was in public, the more likely another incident would be. Sooner or later, it would lead to her exposure. She didn't think she could handle any more stress, she was only just holding herself together as it was. Collecting herself, she forced her mind to focus.

"Reverend, if we could sit down somewhere private?"

Distractedly, the reverend rose and led Netty into his personal sanctuary. Pulling out a chair for Netty, he sat behind his desk.

"Forgive me, my dear, I am a bit preoccupied. Is there something I can do for you?"

Netty hesitantly spoke of her problem, omitting her rape and the loss of their baby. She just didn't think she was strong enough to speak about it and wanted all the reverend's attention directed to the problem with Wil.

"Well, my dear, I do not know how much I can do for you, but I do know that your young man is entitled to bail, as long as he has not been brought to trial as a horse thief. Can you afford to pay bail?" Netty quickly nodded her head yes.

"I will do my best to find out how much it is. I suggest you round up the funds and meet me back here tomorrow. We will go to the sheriff together to post his bail. Once he is out of jail, we can find a good lawyer and think about his defense." Reverend Penny appeared to have recovered from the incident at the altar as he suddenly awarded her with a genuine, snake oil salesman smile.

As Netty left the reverend's sanctuary she felt his eyes bore into her from behind, his change in demeanor fostering a premonition, forcefully banished as she hurried home.

Chapter 8

Wil tried to roll over on his cramped metal bunk bed. He shared his dismal nondescript cell with two other men. His first cellmate had stupidly tried to sell his homemade moonshine to a saloon owner already supplied by Robert Doyle's men. He'd received a severe beating for his efforts and sixty days in jail. Wil wondered what they'd charged him with. The other man was new, moved suddenly into Wil's cell the night before. The big ugly guy kept his silence, sitting on the edge of his bunk staring at Wil, unnerving him.

Wil worried constantly about Netty. He was convinced she was in danger. Why go to these lengths to frame him? And if Netty was in danger, then so was Baby. It was clear to Wil that Robert Doyle wanted the farm and found it expedient to get Wil out of the way first.

He wondered about Netty's mental state. He should never have left her side. In the almost three weeks since his assault and Maggie's murder, time had passed as fast as a snail running a foot race. As of yet, no one had bothered to take the time to inform him of the charges against him. He figured it must have something to do with the gold coins they'd found in his back pocket when they'd searched him after Doyle's men had dragged him to the local sheriff's office. God only knew how the coins had got there. He'd offered nothing when questioned about them.

He didn't doubt for an instant that Robert Doyle had concocted a tidy fairy tale for the sheriff after planting the coins in his pocket. Sadly, no one wanted to hear anything about Maggie's murder. They just ignored him. He still cried whenever he thought about her. In his heart he knew he bore the responsibility. He tormented himself with the knowledge that his poor judgment and immaturity had led to her death and this cell, leaving Netty and Baby vulnerable. *Stupid,*

stupid, stupid. Twenty one years old and sitting in jail with his life still waiting to be lived. His mama would be ashamed.

Underestimating Robert Doyle, the twisted and pernicious bastard, might have cost them their lives. But how could they keep him in here forever? Sooner or later, he would figure out how to get a message to Netty. Maybe he could work something out with his bunkmate when he'd finished his sixty-day sentence.

It was almost time for their dinner. Meals were the only time Wil felt close to Netty and Baby in this cheerless, oppressive lockup. He was reminded of Netty's laughter, her lovely face, her worshiping trust as she stood in the kitchen cooking for him. And boy, everyone knew Netty sure could cook. It had become the nicest part of his day as he reminisced about how they loved to linger over their tea, dreaming big about their plans for the farm, watching Baby wobble around and laughing at his antics before they retired to the bedroom to lie in each other's arms. They marveled about their chance meeting in the woods that had led them to such complete contentment, even as they fumbled with the problems associated with their bodies' changes. Fate is a wonderful thing.

Wil heard noise in the corridor, presumably the trays for dinner. The bailiff appeared at the door to his cell, opening it up with his noisy ring of keys. Surprisingly, he shouted for Wil's bootlegging cellmate, ordering him to accompany him and refusing to disclose further information. Wil casually wondered at the significance of the unusual time chosen to remove his cellmate. The guards knew better than to come between a prisoner and his chow.

Wil's cellmate never returned, nor did they get their dinner. Wondering what was up, Wil turned over in his bunk, lying flat to alleviate the constant ache in his lower back, his tail announcing its growth. Staring up at the drab mucky ceiling, he lost himself in his memories of Netty and Baby.

Wil was so deep in thought that he failed to notice the bailiff quietly returning and silently slip something lethal and shiny to his remaining cellmate. He also failed to notice his cellmate creep slowly over to his bunk, raising the arm that held a glittering butcher's knife and bringing it down solidly on Wil's arm, severing his hand below the wrist, then quickly exiting through the cell door and clicking it shut behind him.

As Wil fell out of his bunk, incomprehension overriding shock, he discovered his severed hand lying on the dirty cement floor. Stumbling to the cell door, he watched the blood stream out of his arm. Sliding down to the cold floor, he held his arm up, hoping to slow the gushing blood.

"Help, I need help. *Bailiff, guard*, please help, I need a doctor. It's urgent. *I'm bleeding.* Help me!" Wil screamed for attention for twenty minutes. No one came. As he slipped further down to the floor, he felt darkness intrude into the edges of his vision. His thought process slowed, blood loss causing him to forget where he was, his arm, now in his lap, cold and painless from shock.

He thought he could smell the warm organic odor of Netty's barn. It must be time to saddle Maggie and turn out the Jerseys. Where was Baby? He couldn't leave without his little buddy in the saddle.

He called for his mama, feeling an urgent need for her soothing hands and loving voice. Slipping into darkness, the last thing reflected in Wil's dimming eyes was the unusual iridescent color of his blood as it finished spilling his life onto the cruddy concrete floor of his cell.

Netty hurried home after leaving the Baptist church. Relief and hope coursed through her body as she rejoiced over the fabulous solution Reverend Penny had suggested. Now all she had to do was find the money. Rushing home with the wagon, she found Baby in the barn with his kittens.

"Baby, I thought I told you to not open the cabin door. It is for your own safety." Scooping Baby up under her arm, kitten and all, she ran to the front door of the cabin, finding it locked.

"Baby, how did you get out of the cabin if the door is still locked from the inside?" Walking around the back, she saw the opened bedroom window. "Well, Baby, I guess this is the way we are going to have to get back in. I am going to boost you up and you can go around front and let me in." Auras sent pressure to her mind.

"Sister, my kitten."

"Yes, Baby, you can take your kitten with you." Shaking her head with amusement, Netty helped Baby through the window and passed the kitten over the windowsill. Going around to the front of the cabin she found Baby waiting for her. She realized Baby had given her the first laugh she'd mustered in weeks.

Dashing through the house looking for money, she happily explained to Baby that Wil would soon be home. Baby trailed behind her with his wobble and shuffle, dangling his kitten from his arm. Counting the money, she realized it might not be enough. *Oh, no.* They'd spent all their savings on the new bakery. *Think, think, think.* She slapped herself on the head. *Wait.* Did she dare?

Running into the bedroom, she dug to the bottom of the hope chest Wil had made for her on the anniversary of their first year together and, ironically, one of Baby's favorite hiding places. She kept digging down till she found it. Withdrawing her fingers, she held up the gold coin. The very one she'd stolen from her husband before she ran from him over three years ago. It would finally do her some good.

Fixing a sketchy dinner for herself, although she found she couldn't eat a thing, she decided to give the cabin a good cleaning. Tomorrow would be a big day. Taking the money to Norristown, Reverend Penny planned to bail Wil out of jail. Counting on their return in a day or two, Netty hoped to celebrate with Wil and Baby before they found an attorney and settled in to resolve the problems with Robert. Cuddling in bed with Baby (and his kitten, of course), she thought about their lost infant. She promised herself to take the time to visit the grave with Wil when he got home. Knowing they both enjoyed excellent health and had youth on their side, she realized that, in time, they could try for a baby again. She finally had her first nightmare-free sleep in weeks.

Rising early, Netty started for town with high expectations. She arrived at the Baptist church shortly after morning service, finding

Reverend Penny in his private office.

"Reverend, I have the money for Wil's bail." She breathlessly poured the coins out on the desk. Looking up, surprised by the reverend's pained expression, she felt her stomach give an uncertain lurch.

"My dear, please sit down. I have some unfortunate news for you." Holding tightly to her hands, he broke the news of Wil's death. Found in his cell, he'd apparently managed to cut off his own hand on the rough metal supports of his bed in an attempt to take his own life.

Netty heard nothing but white noise after the word death. She sagged, dropping heavily to the floor, only held up by the grip Reverend Penny had on her hands. Her head swam. "Oh no, no, no, no, God. Please, no." She moaned as Reverend Penny dragged her to a chair, propping her up.

"*I don't believe you. I need to see Wil,*" she suddenly screamed, hysteria now a frequent visitor.

"I'm afraid we might have another problem on our hands, Mrs. Doyle," the reverend said, releasing her hands. Netty didn't respond. She couldn't make out anything further the reverend said. Her life had just turned to cold ash. This couldn't possibly be true. Wil would never do such a thing. It had to be a lie. She rose slowly, gripping the side of the chair, her face devoid of color. She needed to be alone. Baby; she needed to get home to Baby. She stumbled unsteadily.

"Mrs. Doyle." At the sound of her name, she tried to focus. Reverend Penny stood in front of her, a most pious look on his face, holding his hand outstretched to her. As she reached for his hand, she stared and let her own float in the air aimlessly before dropping it to her side, her defeated countenance a mask of despair and tragedy. For in the palm of his hand lay her gold coin.

Looking into his face, her voice trembling, she asked, "Reverend Penny, what is the meaning of this?"

"Mrs. Doyle, why don't you come with me to the sheriff's office where we can straighten this out? Mr. Doyle himself took time from his precious schedule to come all this way to help us." His grip felt like iron as he tried to ease her toward the door.

"Mr. Doyle?" Netty's saliva stuck thickly in her throat.

"Yes, he is a great benefactor to the church. I thought it best to turn this delicate matter over to him. He usually rewards the church well for the efforts I make in managing the congregation. You understand what I mean?" Netty tried to break Reverend Penny's iron grip on her hand.

"Now, Mrs. Doyle. Why don't you show me what a lady you are and come along?" The reverend sounded exasperated. He snaked both of his arms around her as he relentlessly duck-walked her to the door. Netty suddenly dropped to the ground, releasing herself from his grip. She slipped out from under his arms, grabbed the gold coin, and ran.

Her breath came in gasps as she jumped into her wagon and took off out of town. *Robert is here. What will they do to me? Can they still arrest me? Like Wil? Oh my Lord, what have they done to him?* She refused to believe he was dead until she saw for herself. She'd better plan to hide out somewhere first.

She must get home quickly. Baby waited there. She couldn't run without him. Frantically, she wondered where they could hide. Nothing came to mind. Pitifully, the tears streamed down her face again; her mind so full of panic over Wil and Baby that her adrenalin almost incapacitated her. She drove the horse faster, bumping dangerously over the rutted road.

Netty finally made it to the cabin. She planned to pack food and clothes in the wagon, then grab her Winchester and Baby last. She pulled the wagon right up to the stoop. Banging on the door, she screamed for Baby. As she slipped through the door she turned to close it, glancing toward the barn. She almost fainted at the sight of a dozen men streaming out of the barn toward the cabin. Amongst them, she saw none other than Robert, Eli, the sheriff, Mr. Simpson and the other thugs who worked for Robert.

She quickly locked the door, grabbing her Winchester. Her mind felt pressure, frantic colors swirling wildly in her mind.

"Sister, trouble comes."

"Yes, Baby, we are trapped."

"Where is Brother, he will save us?"

Netty choked back a sob, her trembling hands running spastically through her hair at her temples. "No Baby, we must save ourselves." Dashing into the bedroom, Netty spotted the window. She grasped at an idea. Instructing Baby to burrow under her clothes in the hope chest, she closed it tight. Shoving Robert's gold coin into her pocket, she ran to the window and clambered out. She knew they would realize what she'd done, but at least it would decoy them away from Baby. Running toward the woods behind the cabin, she prayed to God to grant her enough strength to elude the men long enough to get safely to her granite rock. The cavern beckoned; a perfect sanctuary. She knew if she carried Baby with her, she ran the risk of slowing herself down, exposing them to capture. Now, if they did catch her, at least Baby would be safe. After waiting them out, sneaking back to the cabin to collect Baby would solve everything for now. They could hide out at the cavern until she came up with a better plan. Actually, maybe hiding there indefinitely might work out. She didn't eat much anymore and Baby didn't eat food anyway. Water was a small necessity she would worry about later.

Netty made it to the woods without being seen. She heard shouts coming from the direction of the cabin. They must have searched her bedroom by now and found the open window. She'd hoped to have a little more time. Plunging through bramble bushes, she felt them tear her skin. By the time she glanced down to her arms, the scratches had disappeared. *Wow, do I not need Baby to heal me now?* Hope sprang up and lodged firmly in her throat as she ran on.

Trees whipped past, their swaying branches witness to her stumbling; her frantic wits trying desperately to hold her together. Sounds of shouting filtered through the woods like dappled sunlight through the trees. They sounded as if they might be gaining on her. She tried to pick up her pace.

Rounding a corner without watching her footing, she tripped on a rock and down she went, losing her grip on her Winchester. *Damn. Where is the darn thing?* Netty spotted it, victim to her untimely fall, lodged between two rocks. Tugging on it ineffectively, she found her strength deserting her. Precious time lost. Making the decision to leave it behind, she ran on.

Her pace slowed as she located the pathway that ran along the hillside leading to the rock. She remembered pausing to rest here the night she'd discovered Baby. Stifling a sob, she thought about all the happiness he'd brought to her barren life, and to Wil's. She pushed all thought of Wil away. She couldn't afford to deal with her heartbreak now.

Netty navigated the path until she came to her rock. Finally, she found a safe second to pause, forcing painful gulping sobs down her throat. Reaching into her pocket, she withdrew the gold coin. Bitterly, she thought about the trouble her impulsive decision to steal it had rained down on her. Suddenly, flashing auras with their accompanying pressure assaulted her mind. She felt strangled cries. *Baby, oh no.*

"Sister, bad Brother. *Bad Brother, bad Brother.*"

Netty's heart fell. *Is Baby warning me or is he in danger himself?* She slowly turned. It was Eli. He held her Winchester in his hands. Netty felt frozen to the rock. Only a few steps to freedom and it damnably eluded her.

"Where ya go'n, sweetie? Ain't ya happy ta see me?" Leaping forward, he grabbed Netty's ponytail, painfully yanking her back toward the trail. She stumbled and fell, hearing Eli curse her. Her hand reflexively opened, accidentally releasing the gold coin. She could hear it as it bounced from rock to rock, finally settling out of sight near the cairn marking the entrance to the cavern.

"Get yer ass movin' now, Netty gal. He's not a patient man."

Netty saw the glee dancing in Eli's eyes. She pulled herself to her feet, trying to keep up. She knew her chances of escape were now limited. As they neared the edge of the woods, they were joined by more of Robert's men. Judging by the shouts and nasty laughter, she knew they were looking for blood. By the time they cleared the woods, she was being dragged on the ground by three men, her tail bumping painfully over the rocks. Hauled upright, she found herself back at the cabin in front of her barn, Baby, thankfully, nowhere in sight. In front of her stood Robert, holding something wrapped in a handkerchief.

"Well, Netty, it's been a long time. I hear you have something of mine." He glanced around to his men, a depraved grin on his spiteful face. "Well now, I just might have something of yours." He released the handkerchief, allowing it to open before tossing it on the ground. Out rolled a human hand, stiff and gray, clearly severed from a human wrist. Netty could see the telltale signs of iridescent blood soaked into the handkerchief. Soundlessly, she collapsed to the ground, her futile denials confirmed.

When she came out of her faint, Netty found her hands tied behind her back as she stood on the back of her very own wagon, her horse in his traces, prancing nervously. She felt something heavy around her neck. Looking up, she saw a rope thrown over the cross support over her barn door. The very rope attached to the noose weighing down her neck.

"Don't worry about the farm, Netty. I will take good care of it, just the way we took care of your wop drifter." Stepping closer to the wagon, he gave her a wink. Netty strained, leaned over and spat in his face. Wiping his face with his sleeve, Robert shouted for the sheriff. "Alright, Sheriff, I have determined the honor will be yours."

As the sheriff approached, a loud bang came from the stoop of the cabin. It was Eli. He'd one hand wrapped around Baby's crown of crystal antlers, holding him high in the air. The other held Baby's kitten by its neck.

"Look what I found in the bedroom. The weird fucker mus' be her pet." Netty's mind felt a chaotic aura.

"*Sister, bad Brother,* all bad Brothers."

Netty screamed.

The last thing she saw as the sheriff slapped her horse with his hat, jerking her in the air to snap her neck, was Eli. He put a bullet into the kitten's head on the stoop and, tossing Baby to the ground as he jumped, landed on Baby's head with a crunch, spilling his glorious iridescent blood in the dirt before lifting his boot to her stoop, wiping off the essence of the incredible creature that she and Wil had loved so much.

Silence descended over the crowd. The men stared at Netty's limp body as it twisted from the noose, her weight causing the wooden barn support to creak eerily. In the distance, wheels of the wagon rattled mournfully over loose stones as Netty's horse nervously stamped, unattended.

"All right, the show's over. Someone cut her down, for Christ's sake." The sheriff grimaced as Netty's body struck the ground in a heap, her skirt flipping up to reveal a cooling leg.

Eli sheathed the knife he'd used to cut the rope, bending over to nudge the skirt higher.

"Anyone want to peek at the goods? I already had my share." He looked around, sickness drooling from his rheumy eyes.

Mr. Simpson joined him to stare down at the body. Lifting the skirt with the toe of his boot, he stared. "You better come take a look at this, boss."

Robert, the sheriff and the rest of the men gathered around the body. The sheriff slapped Simpson's hand away as he held up her skirt. "Have some respect, you moron. Has she not suffered enough?" His face registered the disgust and revulsion of their actions. Siding up to him, Robert shot him a deceptively casual glance.

"Sheriff, anytime working for me gets to be too much of a burden, you just let me know. I got five or six different men that might just kill for your job." Roberts's cold eyes and chilling tone spoke volumes. The sheriff's expression shut like a slammed door. Stepping back, he glad-handed Robert forward.

"Now, what do we have here, Eli?" Robert bent over. Eli's face drained of color as he booted the body on to its back.

"What the fuck?" All heads swiveled together, leaning in to stare as Eli exposed Netty's golden tail, her fur soaked with urine.

"Holy Christ!"

"Devil's work."

"She's a freak."

"She was your wife, Robert, did you not know about this?" His men looked at him with suspicion. Robert looked from face to face seeing derision.

"Boss, there's sumin' fishy about that pet a hers."

"Go get it, Eli, and bring it over here."

Eli ran to the stoop of the cabin where Baby lay dead in the dirt. Grabbing the carcass by the tail, he returned to the men, tossing it on top of Netty's body. Baby's long leather arm landed on the side of Netty's face as if in a caress. The men were dumbstruck. The tail on the creature matched the tail on the body. Slowly, the men edged back.

"That is just not normal." Robert's face looked as if carved in stone. The rest of the men muttered to themselves, fear-tinged voices threatening to bolt.

The sheriff stepped up to Robert, placing his hand on his shoulder reassuringly, his voice shaky. "Something happened here, for sure. We will never know what. Let's just get them buried and get out of here before a neighbor wanders by. We can come back after the sale of the first acreage closes. I will send someone out here to bring the livestock into town. I know a guy down near Lafayette that will take them off your hands."

Robert didn't respond, but continued to stare at the bodies. The sheriff nodded his head, sending Robert's men scurrying to the barn for picks and shovels. "Make sure you dig away from the house. Go behind the barn. Don't want anyone seeing a grave being dug."

The men returned with their equipment. Stealing furtive looks at Robert's icy demeanor, they grabbed the two bodies, dragging them through the dirt, Netty's head with its broken neck bumping forlornly in the dust.

Locating a likely spot, the men hurriedly dug the grave, then tossed the bodies unceremoniously on top of each other. As they all gathered around for a last look, the sheriff took the time to survey the wide range of emotions displayed at the lip of the grave: fear, disgust, wonderment, greed, and, from Robert, finally hatred.

"Cover 'em up, boys." Robert's voice grated with harshness and animus. Turning on his heels, he headed to the horses. Shouting back to the men, he instructed, "Simpson, hitch your horse to that wagon and bring it back to town with you."

"Yeah, boss." Turning back to the grave, Simpson spat, phlegm landing on the back of Netty's now filthy and tangled golden hair. "Okay, let's finish the job." Bending to their task, the only sounds heard were the grunts of the men and the relentless drop of soil as it swiftly and efficiently covered all signs of the tragic pair that lay in the cold unyielding ground, one hand from each having landed as if reaching for the other.

She felt as if she were floating, drifting, the void enfolding her in its oddness, giving her refuge. It was a good feeling; a blessed warmth surrounding her. The silence seemed unfamiliar. She was unsettled as she could not determine if she were sleeping or awake. She paused. *How can that be?* Assessing her body parts, she realized she couldn't feel them. Wiggling her fingers didn't help; she couldn't feel them, either. She gulped, swallowing. *Wait.* She couldn't feel herself swallow. This was a frightening thought, but she didn't *feel* frightened. A sense of deliberate calm prevailed in her mind. Wow, she was never this calm. *What is going on? Where am I? And why the heck am I so calm?*

She tried to recall her last memory. Something told her not to go there. Alarmed, she pushed through. She wanted to know. But she was clearly being blocked. *Am I alone?* She absolutely knew she shouldn't be alone. *My Baby, where is my Baby?* Her agitation increased, the calming atmosphere losing its effect on her. She started to panic. The more she panicked, the more she started to remember fragments of her former life, flashing back to her in a nebulous gossamer drizzle. *Former life?*

Her Baby, her raw nerves shrieked soundlessly. *Please, my Baby.* Abruptly, she felt an overwhelming rush of gratitude. *Gratitude?* Holding on to that sensation for comfort, she greedily reached out to grasp Baby's searching leather hand. She idly wondered why and to whom she should feel this gratitude. She momentously pulled Baby toward her, his golden rainbow eyes all she needed.

And the final reward. *Reward? Where are these thoughts coming from? Oh, praise God! It cannot be.* She felt a strong familiar arm wrap itself around her waist. Tears rolled down her face, even though she oddly couldn't feel them. Her love was here, too. They were together. Everything would be fine. As she reached out in the dark to embrace him, an uncommon glow filled her eyes. Her senses returning, she detected the first scent of sulfur. Then a sound: soft, an omnipotent whisper.

"Yes, my dear, everything will be fine. But you have much to learn. I have much to teach you. And we must prepare for our guests."

Guests? Netty thought frantically, her heart hammering as she tried to see in the dark. *Where is the voice coming from?*

"My dear, please do not struggle, there is no need. You are safe now. Your Baby and Wil are by your side. You are all safe. The life you used to know is your past. All that matters now is your unlimited future. With my minion and Wil at your side, you will become the first Elder. A female Elder. My most blessed. *My most powerful.*"

"But what of my husband and his men? They will find me."

"You have much to understand, my dear. Your enemies are insignificant and unworthy. They will be dealt with. Time is now forever, but is not meant to be wasted. We must be ready. Even though Baby's mission failed, the results will be the same given more time. If there is to be any saving grace from this colossal failure, we need to begin now."

Netty felt her spirit soar. Her body tingled with anticipation and, could it be hope? She felt Wil relax even as she failed to see him. *Can he hear the voice?*

"I have great faith in you, Netty. Just as you have always had faith in me." And on that note, Netty, Baby and Wil's strange new and heroic life began.

Chapter 9

A month passed as Robert Doyle prepared to sell off some of the assets of the farm. He considered leasing the cabin with the barn and bakery as he knew the bakery may be a gold mine to the right person. He found himself begrudgingly admiring the success Netty and her lover had made of the farm. Studying the plans for the bakery, he marveled at the expense they had devoted to its construction. He puzzled over the source of their funding, sorely underestimating the profitability of their backbreaking labors.

As he sat at his partners desk in his elaborate library, his eyes rested on his antique gold coin collection, reflecting on his frustration over the missing coin. He'd offered a pretty penny to anyone who located it. No luck, and most of the men were reluctant to return to the farm to hunt for it, knowing the bodies rested there. He idly wondered if any of his men had confiscated the coin for themselves.

No, he dismissed the thought. Any dealer or purchaser of such a coin would be known to him. Not much occurred in his part of the state without his knowledge and approval.

Glancing at his gold watch, he noted the time. Pressing a button, he rang for his housekeeper. She appeared quickly.

"Sit down please, Martha. I want you to call the carriage house. Have Eli bring the sedan to the front door. Tell him I want the boys to follow us in the truck. We have some work to do. I expect to be home shortly before cocktail hour. Miss Kathryn will be joining me this evening and we will take dinner in the solarium. Please have Cook prepare one of her favorite dishes. We will then take coffee and dessert in here. Miss Kathryn's father will join us after dinner. Please have fresh flowers in both rooms, this is a special occasion. If my plans bear out, you may have a new mistress sometime in the near future. I have had my eye on her for some time, although I have been forced to pretend a platonic interest." Laughingly, he added, "Well, that will not be necessary any longer, will it?"

"It sure will be my pleasure, sir." Martha sat taking notes; her plump, unlined black face impassive. Returning her pencil to the upswept gray knot on her head, she asked, "That be all for the day, sir?"

Without answering, Robert dismissed her with an irritated wave of his hand. Picking up the telephone, he listened for party voices. He still didn't understand why he must share his telephone line with the neighbors. It hardly allowed for discretion. Hearing silence, he dialed the number for Sheriff Hudson. His secretary picked up the phone.

"Put him on." Robert waited impatiently.

"What is it, Robert?" Sheriff Hudson's booming voice filled the line, making Robert hold the telephone away from his ear, wincing.

"Just a reminder about our little appointment. The boys and I will be leaving in ten minutes. I should make it to the farm in about an hour and a half. I still do not understand why you need me there. The boys are quite capable of cleaning out the store house and dirt cellars on their own."

"Robert, I cannot go into it on the phone. Just humor me. You need to see this for yourself."

"All right. Do not be late." Hanging up the telephone, Robert wondered at the tone of Sheriff Hudson's voice. An unfamiliar note had put him on alert. It took a lot to rattle Hudson. The last time he'd heard that tone in his voice, they were at the farm taking care of a little unpleasantness that his mind refused to dwell on. An uncontrollable shiver coursed through him. His soft manicured fingers absently picked at the paperwork on his desk. Realizing his mind wanted to dwell on the incident despite his desire, he jumped to his feet and hurried to the front door to await his sedan.

Arriving at Lily Pond Road, Eli and Robert pulled into the dusty drive, followed by the well-used pickup truck they utilized for their illicit moonshine deliveries. Spotting Hudson's black Ford, they pulled over and parked. Now that Netty's disappearance no longer raised eyebrows, they no longer needed to sneak in on horses. Both Sheriff Hudson's and Robert's flashy vehicles were easily recognized.

Piling out of the vehicles, the men lumbered toward the barn, casting nervous glances around the grounds. Most of them grumbled under their breath, grousing about the need to return, awaking lurid and macabre memories they had vigorously tried to forget.

"Glad you came. I cannot make any sense of what I found. Maybe you can. Follow me." Hudson led the group to the east side of the cabin. Fully protected from the hot summer sun as it disappeared under the western horizon, they spotted a stout and weathered wooden door built into the ground. Robert frowned in surprise, realizing they had stupidly overlooked what probably contained the results of the late summer harvest. Hudson pulled up the door, letting sunlight expose row after row of Netty's fantastic canned goods. The vibrant colors: red, yellow, green, purple, shone behind the glass of their protective jars as the sun sent glints of solar light back into their faces.

Descending into the cellar, Robert saw rows and rows of magnificent fruit standing neatly in huge rattan baskets. The smells were overwhelming. Organic mustiness mixed with apple, pear and peach. He picked up a firm yellow-white peach, the cool fuzz soothing under his masculine hands. *Yes, hands.* He needed both of them to hold one peach.

"My God, this must weigh four pounds." Robert held it to his nose, the scent overwhelming. Could it be any fresher if he'd just picked it from the tree? "I think my housekeeper could bake three pies from just this one peach. Have you tasted them?"

Hudson nodded. "Sweeter and fresher than anything I have tasted in my life."

"Well, that is certainly curious." Robert looked around, picking up a potato that must weigh a full three pounds. He walked the aisles, spotless and well organized. Hefting every new vegetable as he came to it, he estimated they all appeared to be five to six times their normal weight and size. Biting into an apple, he realized it would take three people to eat it, at least. How Netty had produced results like these baffled them both.

"What about the orchard? Have you checked it out? The trees that support fruit this size must be gargantuan." He looked at Hudson, incredulous. Amazingly, Hudson's stoic stare confirmed his investigation of the orchard. The trees complemented the fruit.

"You are not kidding me, are you?" Robert pensively accepted the unbelievable.

"I reckon Netty and her creature possessed some kind of power. What other explanation can you think of? The popularity of her pies and meat cakes, loved by almost everyone in the town, confirms the unusual qualities of the fruit. What other explanation can there be? Need I remind you how she looked?"

"I do not know what this means, but she did not look anything *like that* before she swiped my coin and took off."

"Well, what do you want me to tell the boys?" Hudson waited patiently as Robert paced. He detested mysteries. Staring at the cellar's miraculous produce, he finally made up his mind.

"Have the boys load up the truck. Make sure they leave nothing behind. Take what you want for yourself, no sense letting it rot. Put some fruit in my vehicle. Sell the rest." He started up the stairs. As an afterthought, he turned. "Yeah, you better drop off a load for Simpson. He'll bitch like a woman if we leave him out." He continued his climb out of the cellar, the treads of the stairs creaking under his weight. Blinking and squinting in the bright sun, he rudely ignored the men standing expectantly at the opening to the cellar. Turning on his brightly polished boot heels, he strolled to his vehicle.

Watching from the front seat of the sedan, his eyes absently followed the movements of his men, monotonously emptying the root cellar. The truck filled rapidly, the men obviously in a hurry to leave. Something in the back of his mind bothered him, but he couldn't put his finger on it. It began to eat at him as he continued to watch the loading. Frustrated, he got out of the car, pacing frantically as he tried to pin down the source of his irritant.

His blood began a slow simmer, his attention focused on an easy target. Netty. She'd done this to him. She'd turned him into a laughing stock with his men. He'd often heard the whispers and crude jokes at the carriage house. He glanced up at them catching a few sneaky peeks in his direction. The fact that Netty had successfully turned this dump into a prosperous economic success burned him even more. He felt like spitting on her grave, the bitch. Shouting to Sheriff Hudson, he motioned for him to join his march to the back of the barn.

"Robert, you do not want to go back there." Hudson ran hard to catch up. "Please, leave it alone. We should get out of here."

Robert threw Hudson a scornful look as he approached the grave. Startled, he froze at the edge. The grave looked caved in. *Son of a bitch, how could that happen?* His face turned crimson, his fists balled in anger. He slowly breathed in and out, trying to keep a lid on his explosive temper.

"Go get the boys. And some shovels, *now*."

Hudson hurried away, shaking his head as Robert stared down at the impossible.

Moans of reluctance announced the arrival of his men bearing the shovels. They gathered at the edge of the grave, snorts of dismay and shock professing their surprise. The silence grew restless, the baffled men unmistakably spooked.

"This had better not be a joke." Robert's ice pick eyes drilled deeply into those of his men. Not a one uttered a sound, more intimidated by Robert than the meaning of the disturbed grave.

"You, you and you," Robert directed in a glacial voice. "Get down there and start digging. I want all of this dirt removed. All of it." His voice started to leak telltale drips of hysteria. Swallowing, he kneeled at the side of the grave, desperately examining the dirt as it flew from the grave to land nearby. Grasping at straws, his face murderous, he turned to Hudson.

"I trust we do not have a case of grave robbery here. I suppose the freak value of the bodies would be worth a few coins." Venom and suspicion leaked from his clenched teeth.

"Please, Robert, for the last time. Let's go. This place might be cursed."

"Now you sound like an asshole, Hudson. *Just shut the fuck up.*"

Sheriff Hudson's face blanched, looking as if he suddenly realized the snail he'd swallowed was still alive. Snickers could be heard from some of the men, hidden protectively behind strained coughs.

"Hey, boss, can we come back up?" The voice from inside the grave convulsed with panic. Robert leaned over the grave as his men scrambled up, not bothering to wait for a response.

"Ain't nothing down there no more; just a bunch of big holes tunneling to who the hell knows where. Looks like they were still alive." The other men joined a chorus of agreement.

"*Shut up, you idiots.* They were dead. The likelihood they dug tunnels to escape is as likely as the possibility I am going to sprout tits in the next two seconds." Roberts's educated mannerisms vanished. Under pressure and attempting to disguise his mounting fear, he sank to the verbal dirt with the rest of them.

"Give me that." He yanked a shovel from a pair of hands, jumping into the grave himself to investigate. He immediately felt a change in temperature. Astonished at the quick chill, he rolled down the sleeves of his white linen shirt, surveying the tight space. As his men claimed, four holes carved darkness into the walls of the grave. Leaning down, he could feel a slight draft of frigid air, smelling a lot like sulfur. The holes were perfectly round, about two feet wide. The soil at the lip of the holes looked burnt and tightly compacted. As he reached down to dig at the compacted soil, his hand dipped into something soft and gooey. Springing back with a girlish scream, he frantically rubbed the substance on his pants. It dissipated, leaving no trace, not even a moist stain. He drew a hand to his heart, feeling it pummel his chest.

Breathing deeply, he steadied his pulse before mustering the courage to peer into the holes again. Adjusting his eyes to the darkness, he located the gooey substance. It encompassed the entire circumference of the hole. The thick and viscous substance appeared to undulate. *Ugh. Is it alive?* Without warning, the substance contracted and withdrew into the hole like an arm being pulled through a sleeve. He lost his balance, falling on his butt in the dirt. He sat stunned. *What the fuck did I just see?* As his wits returned, he started to grasp the vulnerability of his precious butt. He currently sat at the bottom of a grave previously occupied by his murdered freak of a wife and her similarly dispatched nightmare of a pet. Scrambling, he stood, heedless of the cold soil still clinging to his normally impeccable attire.

"Give me a hand, for Pete's sake." Extending his arm, they hoisted him up out of the empty grave.

"What did you see down there, Robert? We heard you scream." Sheriff Hudson brushed at the soil clinging to Robert's pants.

"Do you mind?" He slapped Hudson aside, his natural annoyance masking his reaction to the frightening discovery. "I saw nothing. The bodies are gone because one of you bastards stole them." Deflecting from his own cowardly behavior, he went on the offense. He fixed them with one of his famous ill-tempered scowls. "I had better not hear about this again. *From anyone. Is that understood?*" He watched as his macho thugs nodded slowly, confusion and fear unwilling companions. Satisfied, he wasted no more time. Pointing, he ordered, "I want this grave filled in, then get the sedan and let's get the hell out of here. Eli, Hudson, let's go." Turning his back on everyone, he almost ran to the sedan, vowing to himself never to come near the farm again.

The ride back to town took forever, the three men clearly burdened with individual thoughts regarding the mysteries of the produce and the empty grave. They left Hudson at his office with nary a word. Ten minutes from home, Robert turned to Eli.

"I want you to take the whole crew and any equipment necessary back to the farm, this weekend. Cut down every tree in the orchard, down to the roots. Then burn them; every last one. Burn any berry bushes you find." His expression impassive, he turned to Eli. "And burn the cabin while you're at it."

"I got it boss, but the orchard? We might be able to make some good bucks off that fruit. And the seeds could be really valuable if they matched the results she got. We could get a fancy penny for the new bakery if you throw in the orchard." Eli's homely mug revealed a spark of intelligence previously overlooked by Robert. Impressed, he strove to take a gentle tone. He clapped Eli softly on his mule-like shoulder.

"Seeds, you say? Hmmm, how mindless of me. Search the outbuildings until you discover where her seeds are stored. *And burn them.* I want all evidence obliterated. When the job is complete, you may join me in the library for a brandy while you make your report. You do understand, don't you, that we will never speak of my departed wife and her devilry again?"

"Yeah, boss. I get it." As Eli turned into the gravel drive of Sunnydale, Robert admired the solid comfort and confidence of the magnificent mansion. As ostentatious as some may think it, his home represented the security and normal, quantifiable sanity of his life. Tipping the back of his hand to Eli as the sedan departed for the carriage house, he stepped into his elegant foyer. Its Waterford crystal chandelier swayed amiably, another welcoming affectation of his privileged life. As if a switch had been flicked, he felt transformed. Smug pleasure strengthened his posture as he loudly called out to Martha, announcing his return and depositing all memory of his late wife's, shall we call them, *peculiarities?* into the callous dustbin of his brain.

Eli wiped the back of his chalky lips with a sweaty paw. He was dog tired and as thirsty as a squalling babe searching for its mother's swollen tit. His muscular frame ached from the exertion of the last two days, but they'd actually completed the job on schedule. Of course, hiring a dozen extra hands had helped. He surveyed the field, the waste was pitiful. His men, spent and hungry, hurried to light the bonfires. He planned to let them burn down by nightfall when they'd become more noticeable. He didn't think the boss would appreciate it if the adjoining farmers came poking around his business.

He blew his nose into his hand, slinging it to the ground as he remembered his orders to locate and burn the seed supply. Absently wiping his hand on the back of his canvas work pants, he ambled down the road and up the hill to the barn. He stood under the very wooden support used to hang Netty as he stood wearily looking around the cool interior. The sweet aroma of cow manure, fresh hay and dried horse sweat still permeated the empty barn. No way did they use the barn to store the large quantities of seed he'd expected to find. Not enough room.

Turning away, he hawked dryly on to the ground, berating his rotten luck. Now he would have to tramp behind the cabin to the distant outbuilding near the bakery that he suspected held the seeds. *Sheeit.* Having spotted a few rattlesnakes in the stone wall along the orchard, he knew the field might harbor a few late lurkers as they lay ready to ambush unsuspecting field mice.

Sighing out loud, he shook his head and picked up the jar of petrol he planned to use, simplifying the ignition of the fire. *Okay, let's go break that bitch,* he groused to himself, pathetically trying to gin up some energy for the trek.

It didn't take long to cross the deserted field. The hot sun, now low in the western sky, failed to reach the eastern part of the field behind the cabin, making the large but almost windowless shed appear foreboding and gloomy.

Spotting a fallen tree branch, he fashioned a torch out of dried grasses held together by his pocket handkerchief, which he'd soaked in petrol. Admiring his cleverness, he pulled out a book of matches and lit the torch, grateful for the bright light. Holding the torch high, he pulled the stubborn door wide, juggling his torch and the jar of petrol.

Scanning the storage space, he spotted enormous black earthen jugs near the only window in the place, its panes filthy and useless. The jugs lay on their side in disarray. Curious, he made his way to the window, kicking aimlessly at the jugs, all of them empty. Husks crunched underfoot as he realized someone had beaten him to the seeds. As his torch cast suggestive shadows on the walls, lovers entwined in macabre antics, he considered his next move. Distracted, he felt the shadows mock him as he pondered a plausible story for the boss.

Deciding to retreat back to the field, he turned to go, spotting a large dark round hole in the corner of the shed. *Was that movement?* Eli leaned over, holding his torch high, the jar of petrol safely clutched tightly to his chest. Peering into the corner along the floor, he failed to spot anything. His eyes lifted off the floor to study the hole. It looked familiar. His neck prickled with a persistent feeling of surveillance.

He slowly started to back up, telling himself he needed to get out of there anyway. Turning, his eyes swept up to the ceiling; the sight stopping his heart in mid beat. The thick fibrous and glistening *thing* hung in the air like a slobbering viper preparing to strike. He froze. As his brain registered the fact that the *thing* projected from the round hole, he remembered where he'd last seen identical holes. His bowels loosened, soiling his work pants. As the stench filled the shed, he thanked God for the torch.

The *thing* appeared to study the fire as it hung in the air over his head.

"That's right, you freaky mother fucker. Don't like the fire, do ya?" His courage elevated a notch as he continued his retreat, clutching the torch higher. The torch suddenly threw off a spark, and the *thing* jerked back, causing Eli to jerk reflexively. Off balance, he dropped the torch. In his backward panic, he stumbled, losing his grip on the petrol jar, sending it crashing to the floor to explode on the still flaming torch. As fire rushed to the petrol, liberally splashed prodigiously on his soiled pants, his eyes barely registered the *thing* withdraw into the dark hole. Then the fire quickly swallowed his eyelids and he saw no more.

Robert slowly replaced the telephone receiver. He felt as if he'd been kicked in the stomach; shock and disbelief leaving his hands shaking. He picked up the telephone, its weight suddenly ponderous as he dialed the number.

"Let me speak to him, Hilda." He waited for Sheriff Hudson to pick up.

"Hello, Robert. I guess you heard."

"Have you been to the site yet?"

"I am going out there now. I will let you know what I find."

"You had better let me know everything. I am not paying you to hold back information." Robert's voice gave an embarrassing crack.

"What are you worried about, Robert? Think the place is cursed?"

Robert wondered at the undercurrent of bitter amusement in Hudson's voice. Deciding to let it pass, attributing it to the shock of Eli's death, he barked an abrupt goodbye and hung up.

Chapter 10

Sheriff Hudson hung up the telephone after talking to Robert Doyle. Even though the guy was a sanctimonious shit and an evil one at that, he still called the shots. He certainly didn't plan to hold back any information of the disturbing kind, if he found any. No way. Why miss out on an opportunity to personally cause a worthless piece of dog crap some discomfort? He sensed Robert's growing concern over the events at Netty's farm. If you call festering anger and misplaced righteous indignation, *concern*.

Hudson leaned back in the swivel oak desk chair in his office at the station. Hearing the familiar squeak of the springs gave him a reminder of the perpetual admonishment that always accompanied his shame and guilt when he thought of the money he took from Robert to *look the other way.* In for a penny, in for a pound; the longer he took the money, the deeper he sank, until he found covering up murder commonplace.

He'd never understood why Robert had felt the need to rape and murder his mother-in-law when paying a trumped-up social call at the farm. He'd never offered a reason or an apology. Together, they'd concocted the lone gypsy story for public consumption.

The cover stories had become more and more facile as the murders increased. A few farm girls deflowered once Robert and Eli had finished with them, a missing competitor giving rise to a new business opportunity for Robert, and Netty's own death, along with the unfortunate creature she'd kept as a pet that had made the mistake of catching Eli's sadistic eye. And those were just the murders he *knew* about.

He glanced up at the photograph of his family. His wife, Marne, smiled back at him with the same look he'd fallen in love with over thirty five years ago. His eyes paused as they took inventory of his three healthy children, two now grown with young children of their own. He loved them all; even as his heart ached over the exclusion in the photo of his first born, Emily.

Only he and Marne now knew of her existence, his parents and in-laws long passed away. The tears and wrenched guts never stopped, even long after they'd accepted the necessity of putting Em into a caring home which could give her the professional help her condition required. The move to Newtown to take the available position of sheriff followed soon after her placement.

Em thrived at the home, yet had never achieved more than the skills of a five year old. Only the fact that she enjoyed impeccable care in a homey loving atmosphere made the separation bearable. Once a month, Marne packed their bags and off they went to visit Em, six hours away in upstate New York, to spend whatever remained of the weekend with their girl. She would always be their baby, even as she now approached her thirty-first birthday.

They'd made the decision to keep her existence a secret because of the judgmental stigma they thought their other children might be saddled with. Yet it had taken the intervention of Robert Doyle, like the snake in the Garden of Eden, to enable them to pay Em's bills and actually try to have more children. In the beginning he'd asked himself, *Why not? Everyone did it in one form or another.*

He snorted bitterly as he judged himself harshly. What a stupid greedy ass he'd been. Marne didn't know, of course. He'd never be able to face her if she found out. She called him her hero, and his kids thought their father epitomized a good moral man. Little did they know the extent of his mushy clay feet. He'd lost all respect for himself long ago.

Hudson fingered the metal of his sheriff's badge, worn proudly on his shirt; a pathetic disgrace. He reached up, running his blunt fingers through his thick white hair, still amazingly intact, worrying it until most of the hair stood on end.

He just wasn't sure how much more he could take from Robert Doyle. His neurosis over safely detaching from Robert's malignant clutches completely subordinated the ominous implications of the discoveries made at the farm; the strange and weird parts of Netty's body, her unusual pet and the extraordinary magnificence of her crops.

He tucked the lurking questions away as he prepared to drive to the farm with his deputies to collect the body and start the investigation.

Sheriff Hudson stood in the field behind the cabin as his deputies poked through the wreckage of the shed where Eli's body rested. He held a handkerchief to his nose, a futile effort to block the smell of wet cinder and cooked meat. He ordered Eli's charred corpse remanded to the meat wagon for further examination by the county coroner.

While poking through the paltry carcass of the ruined building, they discovered a round hole in the ground where the outside wall used to stand. With the exception of the charring and it's smaller size, the hole appeared to be a dead ringer to those found in Netty's grave; an unlikely coincidence. Hudson wondered what Eli had found interesting enough to brave walking through a field of rattlesnakes. They had spotted two eastern diamondbacks sunning themselves on rocks as soon as they entered the field.

And what about the hole? Jesus H. Christ, are you kidding me? Something mighty weird and damn serious is going on here. Hitching his pant legs up over his boots, he trudged through the smelly debris to re-examine the hole. Squatting down, he felt the hard burnt edge, wondering what would cause plain ordinary dirt to look as if it had been burned; and only on the edges. He didn't think it had occurred from the fire in the building. The burn was too regular, not natural.

Remembering the holes in Netty's grave, he slid his hand into the hole, rubbing the sides of the wall, feeling wet glopiness. Quickly extracting his hand, he wiped the residue on his handkerchief, carefully rolling the sample and placing it safely in his pocket to send to the laboratory. If he used Robert's name, he could probably get the results back in a week. Not that he expected to find anything worthwhile.

Kicking his feet aimlessly through the rubble, he meandered away from the shed's remains, making his way carefully through the field to his police car. Sliding behind the wheel, he rested his head on the back of the seat, his eyes closed. He felt a shudder of weariness snake through his body. Elusive sleep was playing a mean game of catch-me-if-you-can, tormenting him relentlessly since the murders. He rubbed his tired eyes, enjoying the sensation while refusing to let his mind give credence to the coincidence of the holes. As he started the patrol car, he felt a rumble in his stomach. Not knowing if he wanted to vomit or defecate he pushed the thoughts of horror from his mind and headed to town.

"I have Roger on the line, Sheriff." His secretary stood at his door to deliver the message, her interest in the call ill-concealed, as usual.

"Okay, Hilda, I got it." Picking up the telephone, he heard Hilda softly pick up the extension. No time for delicacy.

"Hilda, can you please give me a little privacy?" Hudson winced as he heard Hilda give an offended "harrumph." But she got off the line.

"Hey, Roger, thanks for getting back to me so fast. Mr. Doyle will be sure to show his appreciation."

"No need, Sheriff Hudson, always happy to help out Mr. Doyle. If he needs anything else, you be sure to let me know, you hear?" Roger's voice oozed so much ass-kissing, Hudson swore his own butt tingled.

"Yes, of course, Roger, now how about those results?"

"Well, Sheriff, that's another matter. I think you need to come to the laboratory. I don't think we should discuss this over the phone."

Impatience crept into Hudson's voice as he informed Roger he had no intention of driving four hours to New York City and then another four hours back to Newtown for some stupid laboratory results. Hudson took a breath, forcing himself to calm down as his voice developed a shrill tone.

"Well now, Sheriff, no need to get all riled up. I am just trying to be discreet, for Mr. Doyle's sake, of course."

Hudson slapped his forehead, his frustration doing a slow simmer. "Roger, can you please just give me the results? Paleeease?"

"Okay, Sheriff Hudson, if you insist. Don't forget to tell Mr. Doyle about my concern for discretion." Hudson rolled his eyes, closing them painfully, wondering when this would end.

"The substance you sent me is organic. I found a system of three types of cells in what I can only conclude is a type of plasma. But there seems to be an absence of white cells. You cannot survive without white blood cells. They fight infection in anything alive. And I am unable to identify the three types of cells present. They do not exist in any species on this planet, yet they are definitely organic. Yes, yes, an organic life form of some type, all very confounding, but not the *most* amazing discovery. By the way, did you see the creature that provided the sample?"

Ignoring the question, Hudson's attention perked up measurably. "Roger. What exactly did you find?"

Lowering his voice to a conspiratorial whisper, Roger continued, "*It had bugs.*" Roger said it as if he'd just uncovered the Holy Grail, his breath resounding loudly through the wires.

"What do you mean, bugs? That's no big deal."

"On the contrary, Sheriff, the bugs were no ordinary bug. They looked like tiny red polliwogs. You know, before they turn into frogs? They are, or I should correctly say *were*, complete organisms, that actually propelled themselves in the plasma."

"Roger, could you make this more to the point? What do you mean *were*?"

"As I said, they propelled themselves. Yes, yes! Right out of my office. They are gone, all of them. They rose up from the sample under the microscope, attracting each other like a magnet, and then went flying out my open window. They appeared to swell as they converged, I don't understand why. They were almost microscopic, how could they enlarge like that? When I re-examined the sample, the only thing left was a smeary residue."

Hudson didn't know what to think. He felt calm yet his heart thumped wildly. What the heck did all this mean?

"Sheriff, are you there?"

"Yes, Roger. Thanks for your help." Hudson prepared to hang up, ignoring the last of Roger's words.

"The creature, Sheriff; what about the creature? Did you—?"

Silence descended as Hudson replaced the telephone, Roger completely forgotten.

He sat at his worn desk trying to make sense of recent events. Two missing bodies, Eli's mysterious death by fire, sinister holes at both scenes and now the baffling, yet ominous, laboratory results. The time had come to inform Robert. He wondered if he could get away with a phone call instead of a command performance. Drumming his fingers restlessly on his desk, he made an easy decision.

With the telephone in hand, he dialed Robert's number, hoping the party line was clear. He wanted to get this over with. Thankfully, Robert picked up. Updating him on the investigation didn't take long. The news about the laboratory results produced an unexpected reaction.

"Did I tell you to mess around with that hole? And what makes you think they are related? Big deal. I do not want to hear any more about Netty, her infernal pet and their tails or these damnable holes. *Do you understand me?*"

"Robert, you need to calm down and listen to me."

"I don't think I heard you correctly, Hudson. Are you trying to tell me how to behave?"

The sheriff felt the ice in Robert's voice seep its pernicious fingers right to his stomach. He needed to tread carefully. "Robert, I understand you just fine. Let me check one more thing. Remember Netty's young drifter?"

"I have no idea what you are talking about."

Losing his temper, Hudson let Robert have it. "I know exactly what you did to that innocent kid, Robert. You didn't have to do it like that, just to get him out of the way. You had other options. You always take the easy way out. Do you think I don't know *everything* that happens in the jail? Or exactly who is on your payroll?"

"Well now, Hudson, looks like you have a bee in your bonnet so why don't you just spill what is on your mind." Robert's demeanor changed so quickly, Hudson's radar went on high alert.

"We can settle the question of coincidence if we check the grave where you buried the kid." Silence greeted the proposal. "Robert? Where is he buried?" Silence. "*Robert.*"

"All right, Hudson. You can check the grave. But you better prepare for some irregularities," Robert sounded off. Where were the confidently arrogant intonations of the old Robert? Something was up, for sure.

"Why don't you fill me in, Robert? The whole story, please."

"Yes, I did have him taken care of in the jail. When the boys came to collect the body, it had already been sent to the coroner's office. He was just a no account drifter, no family. They assumed Potter's Field would be fine for burial."

"Robert, why don't you tell me about the body?"

"Err, yes, the irregularities. It seems the drifter exhibited some of the same strange affectations we found on my unfortunate deceased wife."

"Affectations, that's what you call them? Are we going to continue to dance around this or are we going to start calling a spade a spade? What is it going to be, Robert?" For some reason, prying information out of Robert was like trying to convince a high school virgin to give it away to the school misfit.

"*Alright.* He had a tail. And something was wrong with his blood. It was all over the cell floor and it glowed. It was not red. We discovered something else during the prep for burial. It seems he was growing wings."

"What do you mean, wings? As in to fly? Those kind of wings?"

"Yes." The word came across the telephone wire as a fearful whisper.

Hudson held the telephone to his ear, not doubting what he'd heard, just astonished. It wasn't information that he'd expected. His stomach began to grumble again. A cold sweat broke out on his forehead.

"I need to look at the grave. You know it must be done. Tell me the location so I can figure out what is going on."

"What do you mean, what is going on? There is *nothing* going on."

"Robert, do not give me that. Are you blind? You think Eli's death was an accident? Well, it wasn't. He was not alone in that shed. Now, get me the location so we can deal with this."

"All right, I will get back to you. But do not even think about sharing this information with anyone without my permission or I will have your ass." The old Robert, clearly back in control.

Chapter 11

Sheriff Hudson cautiously eased the police car to the curb in front of the two-story colonial that sat next to his target house. He looked carefully at the target, seeing no one in the neat green yard that led to the cheery white ranch-style home with vibrant flowering window boxes.

Emerging quietly from the patrol car, he held one hand behind his back, the contents hidden. Crouching, he quickly sidled up to the door of the house, finding it unlatched. Peering into the small window in the door, he decided the coast was clear. He slid his big body inside the house, softly closing the door with a loud click. He held his breath, praying the sound didn't carry to the other rooms. He heard the clink of dishes from the kitchen. He would launch his attack from there.

He saw her at the kitchen sink, her back to him. He knew she would squirm like a hungry pussycat if he could get her underneath him. He licked his lips as the nape of her neck inflamed him.

Slowly, silently, he crept closer, his hidden hand coming forward as he wrapped his other arm around her waist, forcing her to face him as his lips descended on to hers; demanding a kiss from the most beautiful woman in his world.

"Ummm, what a surprise. Are these for me?"

"None other, my love." He held out the bouquet of bright multi-colored roses; always her favorite. He looked at Marne's aging face, her smile still wide and bright; every line familiar and safe, and loved. When she looked at him, really looked, and smiled that smile, his heart flipped just the way it had when he fell in love with her so long ago.

"I have the bags all packed. I thought we would eat a quick dinner before we go. It's a long drive." Marne moved from between his arms to hunt for a vase for her flowers. Finishing with the flowers, she whirled to face him.

"I love my roses. You sure do know my soft spot. But hon, would you mind?" Her face radiated a mixture of sweet apology and maternal love. He knew what was coming.

"Can we bring the flowers with us? For Em? She will love the colors." Hudson looked at his wife, tears coming to his eyes.

"Of course, my love, you're right. She will love them." And with that, she stepped back into his loving arms.

As Hudson drove into Em's town with Marne and the roses at his side it was early morning, the overcast sky not yet willing to yield to the demands of the rising sun. They had driven up the night before, staying at a comfortable nearby inn so they could get an early start, wanting to spend as much time with Em as possible before they had to turn around and go home.

Turning into the road to the modest brick group home, they were surprised by fire trucks and police cars with their flashing lights. Parking the car, they hurried into the reception area, encountering Mrs. Post, the housemother.

"Mr. and Mrs. Hudson, I did not expect you so soon."

"Good morning, Mrs. Post. Why are the authorities here?" Sheriff Hudson's tone reflected a passing interest, sure the incident was minor.

"Well, er, perhaps you might join me in my office. I shall ring for the nurse. She will have Emily join us there." Hudson and his wife exchanged startled glances.

"Wait a minute. What is going on? Did something happen to Em?" Marne gripped Hudson's arm tightly, the roses threatening to slip from her hand.

"Please, Mrs. Hudson. Relax. Emily just had a nightmare. Come. We can talk in my office." Visibly relieved, the Hudsons allowed themselves to be ushered into the housemother's cramped office. Settling Marne into an upholstered armchair, Hudson stood behind his wife. Mrs. Post sat at her desk with her hands clasped, her tone sympathetic.

"Last night, Emily woke up screaming. She seemed to be in the grip of hysteria. Calming her down took hours. She refused to sleep in her bed, forcing me to take her to my room where I made space for her in my bed. I hope that you do not find that presumptuous."

"No, no, of course not. Did she say anything about the nightmare?" Marne's concerned voice was laced with confusion.

"Emily actually does not admit to a nightmare, Mrs. Hudson. We just assumed her story arose as a result of a nightmare."

Hudson raised his hand as if to cut off Mrs. Post. "Please tell us exactly what my daughter said." His unexpectedly hoarse voice drew startled glances from both Marne and Mrs. Post.

"Of course, sir." Mrs. Post continued in hurt tones. "Emily's story centered around the claim that a monster wanted to get in her window. She insisted she was not asleep. She said the monster stared at her and took a few swipes at the window before her screams woke us. When we entered the room, we did notice some gunky slop on the window, probably from a large bird smashing itself on the pane. The fact that she is on the second floor convinced us it had been a nightmare."

"Why are the police and the fire department here?"

"That is another matter entirely. This morning, I happened to inspect the back yard, just looking for anything unusual in view of Emily's nightmare. Oddly enough, underneath her window, I found a hole in the ground. It had not been there the day before. The smell of sulfur seemed to rise from the hole. I dropped a pencil into it and could not hear it land. So I called the police. They called the fire department because of the safety issue."

Mrs. Post abruptly rose to her feet. She stared at Hudson, mouth agape. "Sir, are you okay?" Hudson's legs had failed him, forcing him to grab on to the back of Marne's chair.

"Get my daughter in here, *now*." Turning to Marne, who sat with a shocked look on her face, he demanded, "Go pack her clothes; she is coming home with us."

"Honey, what's wrong? You are scaring us."

He put a tired hand on her shoulder. Attempting to force a lighter tone, he let his words silence their questions. "Marne, we will discuss this later. Please pack Em's clothes quickly. We will send for anything else. I want to be out of here in the next twenty minutes."

"Mr. Hudson, this is quite irregular."

"I am sure it is, Mrs. Post. I am sure it is."

All the way back home to Newtown, Marne's questioning pensive eyes weighed him down. She knew they couldn't speak of the matter in front of Em, and would bide her time until they got home. He'd better have a good explanation for her. At the moment, he didn't. God knew, he couldn't tell her the truth.

So he withdrew into himself for the entire six-hour drive. Marne sang nursery rhymes to their thirty-one-year-old daughter as she played in the back seat with her favorite doll.

"But why do you have to go now? Can it not wait until Monday? And you still have not explained this mad decision to bring Em home with us." Marne looked like she was holding tightly to the very last lock on her temper, her patience beyond exhausted.

Hudson closed the door to his closet, his sheriff's jacket in his hands. He sat on the bed next to his wife, putting his arm around her. "Baby, do you trust me?"

"Yes, of course. Why would I not trust you, Hud? Please tell me what is going on. And what does it have to do with Em?"

"Honey, I think it is time to bring Em home and introduce her to the rest of the family. I want you to call the kids and invite them over to Sunday dinner. We need to do this now." He looked into eyes flickering with trust, love, confusion, and was that a hint of fear? It broke his heart to do this to her, but he knew no other way out. He just needed to check one more thing before he made up his mind. He rose to his feet, pulling Marne up with him.

"I love you more than my own life. Do you know that, Marne?"

"Yes, Hud. I knew that the day I married you."

"Is Em still sleeping?"

"Yes, Hud."

"Promise me you will not let her out of your sight."

She nodded her head, the questions still in her lovely eyes. He took a finger and traced the curve of her lips, caressing the side of her face as he bent down for a final kiss. Lifting his jacket from the bed, he turned and left the room.

Sheriff Hudson stood in the cool graveyard, pulling the collar of his jacket tight to ward off the bite of the northern wind that claimed the graveyard as its own. He clutched a piece of paper in his hands; directions to Netty's lover's grave. The poor kid, so needless. He made his way down the rows of unmarked graves, wondering where the boy's family lived and if they'd given up on his return home. Funny, he didn't even know the young man's name.

He followed the directions that led him to a dip in the topography of the graveyard, creating a shallow crater that sheltered him from sight. Not that he had any company, except for the unclaimed forlorn bones of the indigent, nestled in their ignoble final roost.

Hudson counted carefully, following the directions to the correct grave. But he needn't have bothered. He only needed to search for the grave that looked as if a bomb had exploded from the inside. Like the one in front of him. Compressing his lips until they turned white, he leaned over the edge of Netty's young lover's grave, finding it empty; just as he'd expected. Bad time to be right; a very bad time.

Hudson knew he didn't have to bother to look for the expected holes at the bottom of the grave. His nose clearly detected the faint trace of sulfur which he knew emanated from them. Just like the holes beneath the window of his daughter's bedroom. Mrs. Post had fortunately interrupted the monster before it could abduct Emily. Or kill her for the same reason it had killed Eli. *Revenge.* Now the monster appeared to be extending its quest to his family. Why? There must be an unfathomable connection between the monster and Netty's unorthodox family. If the monster just wanted to kill him, opportunities presented themselves every day. Why go after Em?

Hudson suddenly fell to his knees, a germ of a thought,

previously relegated to the recesses of his consciousness, arose mightily to claim its rightful place as the only true answer to his impossible question. It wasn't just revenge. It was *vengeance*. It wanted him to suffer before it killed him. The monster could think and reason. It had a plan. It wanted him to feel pain and loss; just as they'd caused it to feel the pain and loss of Netty, her lover and the unusual creature brutally and callously murdered by Eli. Was that it? *Oh, my God!* Hudson rocked back and forth on his heels as the realization of the danger he'd put his family in hit home. The monster wanted him to suffer by killing *his* family.

A tear escaped a brimming eye as he arose, a resolute solution filling him with regret and sadness. He wiped his face with the back of his hand and started the trek back to his patrol car. One quick stop at his office and he could put an end to the threat to his family.

Sheriff Hudson hurriedly finished the letter to Marne, slipped it into an envelope and held it to his heart. He took a last look around his office, then stepped out to Hilda's desk.

"Hilda, I need you to do me a favor. This needs to stay between us, do you understand?"

Hilda looked blankly at the sheriff. "Of course, Hud, what do you need me to do?"

"I want you to take this letter and give it to my wife."

"Your wife? Don't you want to give it to Marne yourself?"

Sheriff Hudson placed a shaky hand on Hilda's shoulder. "Hilda, I am asking you for a favor that must stay between us. You must promise me. No one else can know."

Hilda frowned, looking searchingly into Hudson's face. She apparently read something in his expression which told her he meant business.

"Sure, Hud, I will be happy to do this for you." She took the envelope, placing it in her purse under her desk as Hudson watched. Turning back to his office, he slowly headed for his desk and closed the door behind him.

He sat down in his worn desk chair, took a deep trembling breath, focused on the photo of his Marne, took out his service revolver, held it to his temple, and pulled the trigger.

Epilogue

Life moved on for all involved in the strange covert murders on Lily Pond Road. Robert's men found their lives initially taking a huge turn in prosperity as he paid handsomely for the silence of his henchmen.

The loss of Eli unexpectedly grieved Robert. The fact that Robert was his employer failed to diminish the rousing camaraderie and confidence they'd shared when executing Robert's despicable and illegal deeds for well over two decades.

He refused to return to Lily Pond Road after his men had reported the fire and Eli's death. A simple telephone call to Sheriff Hudson had directed the matter to his capable hands. Unfortunately, the disturbing results of Hudson's report had terrified him. Putting Netty behind him no longer appeared to be the effortless proposition he'd first anticipated.

The sheriff's death had shocked the entire tri-county area. The day after Robert had relayed directions to the drifter's grave, Sheriff Hudson had returned to his office and blown his brains out with a single shot from his service revolver. He'd left an adored wife, three adult children and two grandbabies. Robert heard unsubstantiated rumors that he'd left his wife a suicide letter with some sort of purported explanation that allowed her to carry on with her head held high, unlike the wife of a man who'd taken the coward's way out.

He would have put a lot of money on a bet that Hudson hadn't had a cowardly bone in his body. *So why the suicide?* And unaccountably, his entire family, including his adult children and their families, had left town for parts unknown after the funeral. *Why the rush? What were they running from?*

A public burial held at the local cemetery had put Eli's body to rest.

Quelling the rise of local gossip, Robert had concocted a simple cover story involving a fall and a fatal rattlesnake bite; hardly original, tediously routine. Not much different than the story circulated to explain Netty's death. Accidents happened every day. People died every day; sad, but unremarkable.

Robert sat in front of the fire in his library, contemplating his future. The emptiness in his life, exacerbated by the loss of Eli, continued to disturb him. The accumulation of wealth no longer interested him. Irrevocably securing his fortune and influence far beyond his dreams, he saluted the plan hatched fifteen years ago when he'd discovered that Netty would become heir to half of the vast Woods' fortune.

He paused to consider how easily the gullible Woods had swallowed Robert's suddenly smitten sensibilities enough to marry a common country waif. Smiling, he remembered how he'd found a few kicks to amuse himself with after the wedding, although her unfortunate broken nose and subsequent hair loss robbed him of his interest in forcing her to submit. *Time to move on. Let me see, what else?* Ticking them off in his head he continued the auspicious list.

His pursuits on the bench no longer interested him. The petty legal problems of the pedestrian public wore him down. Prohibition had soon gone down the tubes. Not that he needed the money, but dabbling with thugs late at night had given him a worthwhile thrill.

He'd even found himself bored with his *special* evenings, the brutality of rape no longer seen as powerful and exciting, now merely churlish and unrefined.

Tapping his finger along the side of his imperial nose, a solution occurred to him; a concept that needed a little feedback. Rising from the sofa, he stuck his head out of the library door into the foyer.

"*Martha, get in here, please.*" An intriguing expression settled comfortably on his haughty features. Crossing to the burled walnut sideboard, he poured brandy into tiny crystal snifters.

"Yes sir?" Martha stood at the library door, the bun on her head unwinding from the heat and labors of her bustling day, her apron wrinkled and stained. Robert grimaced, eyeing the apron.

"Put your apron in the hallway won't you, Martha?" She regarded him with a blank look in her eyes. "The apron, the apron." He waggled his fingers at her, the gesture dismissive. She quickly removed her apron, returning from the hall to stand before him.

"Yes, yes, much better. Please sit down, Martha, I have an announcement." Handing her a snifter, he directed her to the sofa at the fireplace. He took his customary seat at the other end. Martha sat, eyeing the snifter, looking as natural as a defecating woodpecker in her hand. Oblivious, Robert chattered on.

"I have definitely decided to marry Miss Kathryn. I have yet to ask her, of course. But I do not anticipate a problem. It is high time we fill this house with children. As you will agree, she is quite suitable. Drink up, my dear." He again waggled his fingers at her. "Please arrange time, beginning next week, to sit with her to plan the arrangements. Give her anything she asks for. The wedding will be held here, of course." He glanced at Martha, still frozen with the snifter in her hand. "Martha, if you are to be my new major domo, you must learn to relax. Now drink up." Blinking slowly, he watched her raise an eyebrow and bring the snifter to her lips as he continued to happily rattle on about his extravagant wedding and the new direction their lives would take.

The years evaporated quickly. Robert and Kathryn, the toast of Norristown's exclusive social whirl, found branching into New York City society presented many intriguing opportunities. Over the years, he'd converted his vast fortune into the banking business, burnishing his now impeccable reputation. No one ever condescended to peek under the veneer of genteel hospitality to the worm holes and rot in the foundation of his wealth and soul. Not even his wife, Kathryn.

As the joyful celebration of Robert's seventy-third birthday passed, he showed tentative signs of waning strength. He no longer cared to attend the season's social calendar, choosing to closet himself in his library to pass the day.

Kathryn proved to be a loving fertile wife, blessing Robert with five children. Their firstborn son, Garrett, hard at work polishing the chrome of their 1956 Cadillac Convertible, planned to drive the family to Summit. Robert and Kathryn's eldest daughter, Judith, having married at seventeen, needed to return to her home with her baby after enjoying a short visit with the family.

Riotous laughter emanated from the car as they piled in. Robert fondly waved goodbye to his wife and five children from the wide, columned front porch, declining as usual to accompany them. Even though he adored his family, the fact that Judith's husband, Edwin, planned a surprise unveiling of their new home didn't tempt him to join the party.

Robert returned to the sanctity of the library, ringing for Alice to bring him his specially blended licorice tea. Martha, having failed to achieve a modicum of the confidence he used to share with Eli, had retired shortly after Garrett's birth. Perhaps she'd sensed his disappointment in her.

As he awaited his tea, his mind catalogued the many highs of the last two decades since he'd reformed his life and married Kathryn. The list was prodigious. The highlights truly culminated with the birth of Garrett, his favorite son and heir. The boy, almost a copy of Robert at his age, showed promise as a financial wizard, an asset in the banking empire he planned to leave to him.

The only bedbug in the mattress centered around the mysterious deaths, purely a coincidence of course, of most of the men involved in the cover up on Lily Pond Road. Robert had decided twenty years ago to edit the name of his first wife from his memory. He'd even convinced himself that the two thousand acres he'd stolen from her had passed to him legally. Unfortunately, his persistent dreams and sweats had proved to be uncontrollable, refusing to allow him a single untroubled night's sleep.

Eli and Hudson's deaths had only been the beginning. Subsequent deaths befell three more of his men, another shocker. The only thing left of the men he'd sent to the train station to pick up some freight had been their skeletons. No clothes, no blood; just a macabre triangle of desiccated bones lying in the dirt. And, heaping insult on injury, no witnesses. *Son of a bitch.*

"Your tea, sir." Alice placed a silver tray with a filigree teapot and one fine bone china tea cup on to his partners desk.

"Pour for me, won't you, young lady?" The fifty-six-year-old housemaid poured his tea and returned to her duties, leaving him to savor the ambrosial fragrance in seclusion. Ah, yes, small pleasures. He sipped the sweet tea slowly, his face suffused with blood, warmed by the steam of the tea. His thoughts returned to the cause of his woefully inadequate sleep.

The most disturbing death belonged to that of Simpson and his wife. They had regularly worked late in their shop two nights a week with the help of a young female employee. Their bodies had been found behind the butcher's shop near the garbage receptacle. They protruded from a perfectly round hole in the ground which had opened to a small tunnel that had collapsed around the bodies. The coroner's report blamed heart failure, for both of them. When asked, their hysterical employee had claimed she *'never heard nothin'*.

Robert's blood froze in his veins every time he thought about the mysterious holes. He wondered why he remained alive. How long could one withstand relentless stress and sleeplessness? Perhaps his refusal to leave the house protected him. The commonality of the deaths (they had all occurred outside) suggested that he probably remained safe as long as he stayed inside. He could not know for sure, but eleven years had passed since the last death.

Discovering his teapot empty, he rang for Alice, requesting a refill and directing her to serve his dinner.

As he waited for the tea, he happened to glance in the direction of the French doors that led out to the terrace and his glorious emerald lawn. The same French doors Netty had fled through after first stealing his gold coin. *Damn.* He'd promised himself he wouldn't think her name. Concentrating on the glass of the French door, his squinty eyes widened as a looming form quickly disappeared. Was his imagination playing tricks on him? *For God's sake.* Rising to investigate, the shrill sound of his telephone forced him to pause. Distracted, he picked up the heavy receiver, hearing the annoyed voice of his son-in-law, Edwin.

"Hello, Robert, just a quick call. I hoped everyone would be here by now. They are at least fifty minutes late. I wanted to take them to the new house before it got dark. I am surprised at Judith. I made it clear to her she must keep to schedule. Did they depart on time?"

Robert consulted his watch. *Goodness, this is odd.* "Edwin, they left earlier than planned, did Judith not call you? That was almost two hours ago. Perhaps they stopped to shop?"

"Not with the baby with them. She gets fussy before dinner. Judith would never nurse her in public. It is unseemly. Whoops, there is the doorbell, probably them. Sorry to disturb you, Robert. See you soon." And he hung up. From the distance, he heard his own doorbell ring. *Company at this hour?* Ringing the kitchen, he commanded Alice to see to the door.

Anticipating a social visit, Robert ran his liver-spotted hands through his still robust gray hair. He quickly donned his tweed sports jacket, covering the tea stains on his white linen shirt. To his surprise, Alice appeared, escorting two Norristown police officers. Their bearing was tense, their expressions tight.

Robert felt a wash of fear, a growing pain in his right arm. He stood as one of the officers spoke, hearing him clearly, but failing to fully comprehend.

"Mr. Doyle? We are sorry to inform you that there has been a tragic accident involving your family, all dead, skeletons, infant bones, no witnesses, undamaged vehicle, investigation." The voices droned on as Robert's ears filled with a white buzzing sound. His hand clutched at his chest, a feeble attempt to relieve the sudden pressure. As he tumbled over, his pain-glazed eyes hesitated as they registered the specter of the looming mass hanging quietly over the top of the French doors, now undulating with golden striates. As he smashed his face on the corner of his partners desk, the excruciating pain in his fatally damaged heart could not prevent the despairing realization that Netty had somehow managed to save her coup de grace for him.

THE END

Introduction to
Species Intervention #6609
Book 2

Echo

Synopsis for Echo:

Netty's influence transcends a full century as the United States evolves to a point of politically driven economic collapse. The year is 2044 as a young mother, abused by her shiftless husband, heroically decides to remove her two sickly children, Scotty and Abby, from the mean streets of their government subsidized tenement town of Short Hills, New Jersey to the hills and old farmland of Sussex County. There they unite with a Latino family that adopted Jose, a young boy from Costa Rica who was traumatized at the age of seven by the brutal murder of his parents and the kidnapping of his infant sister.

The two families unite to pool finances, creating the love and bonds that will enable them to survive the psychotic attention of Armoni, a soul damaged beyond redemption; discovery of Baby's miraculous offspring, Echo; and their subsequent body changes. Through the efforts of Echo, who develops an unexplained passion for the curly-haired dog, Barney, they flee the clutches of Armoni after the murder of Armoni's sidekicks by Echo, to Sarasota, Florida, one of the last remaining enclaves of wealth in the U.S.

Scotty learns to utilize Echo as a co-conspirator in his intrigue to thwart the efforts of heinous people that prey on the lives of creatures in their environmentally rich new home, where the insidious miscreant, Armoni, tracks them; dragging along Ginger Mae, a New

York City prostitute looking for opportunity with her mute child, Daisy, bringing brutality and violence to all.

Having fallen in love, the young Abby and Jose grow close, only to be separated by the transcendental Netty, who tries to use Abby as a conduit in her plan to rescue as much wildlife as she can before despicable political events bring on the specter of Armageddon.

Bonus Chapters 1-3

Chapter 1

2044 AD

Scotty slipped out his front door unnoticed, easily overlooked if you failed to notice his ringworm and impetigo scars. Barely three and a half feet tall, even at six years old, it put him in the underdeveloped category, another result of the wicked fall his mother had taken while pregnant with him. The fall had initiated his premature birth, keeping him in a grossly understaffed neonatal hospital unit where his tiny body had contracted a number of skin diseases that had left him scarred and disfigured.

To add to his misery, his left eye muscles had not fully developed, allowing his eye to wander in its socket, giving him headaches, vision problems and disfiguring facial effects. The fact that his father continued to deny responsibility for his mother's fall illustrated the truth of his sister, Abby's, claims. His mother had married a full-blown leachy weasel.

Scotty looked up and down the bleak empty hallway, dirty graffitied walls, a testimony to the futility of the lives packed like termites in the ugly utilitarian monstrosity he called home.

He cautiously peeked in the stairwell. Seeing it empty, he scrambled down the cold metal stairs, his tiny worn sneakers masking his footfalls. Emerging from the gloom of the stairwell, he recoiled from the sudden glare of an unexpectedly sunny afternoon.

Scooting around to the back of his building, he dodged empty beer cans, used condoms and piles of dog feces to hide in the big cardboard box he currently used as his fort.

Yesterday, Chang Appliance, the largest Chinese appliance chain in the world, had delivered something to an exceedingly lucky tenant in his building. He and his buddy, Germaine, had quickly claimed the treasured empty box, dragging it to the back of their tenement in the giant public housing neighborhood of Short Hills, New Jersey, hoping they could hide it from the big guys—at least long enough to have some fun with it.

Short Hills, formerly a bastion of affluent homes in the early part of the century, no longer boasted anyone who could afford them. As a result, the Socialized New World Party had strengthened the urban renewal and eminent domain laws. When the real estate market for large expensive homes (the most visible trapping of despised capitalist pigs) collapsed, due to the exodus of the wealthy to more welcoming countries, the homes were appropriated. After removing the squatters and gangs, the bulldozers made way for what some called inevitable progress. The kind of progress that produced nasty government-subsidized housing projects; pretty ironic for a state once known as The Garden State.

Now New Jersey blossomed with one huge hideous urban ghetto after another. Just like many other states undergoing a similar renaissance. Not everyone agreed to call this progress. Like his mother.

She remembered the stories her grandmother had related to her about growing up on a working family farm with cows and hay barns and wide open meadows, replete with the simple harmonies of sunrise crows, twilight crickets and the exceptional fragrance of newly mown grass and wild wood violets.

His great-grandmother had spent her summers as a child delving into the woods, looking for wild strawberry patches and black caps growing along the side of the road, probing water holes and brooks for magical polliwogs, turtles, minnows, even snakes which she invariably dragged back to the farmhouse, a favorite pastime.

Instead, Scotty lived with the perpetual smells of hot air brakes, big rig exhaust and alley rat infested garbage. He heard the sounds of gunshots and screams as the bullies of the neighborhood beat on their latest victim. His playground consisted of hot smelly asphalt and discarded cardboard boxes as his playthings.

Luckily, his mom knew of a few areas that had missed out on the progress. Like Sussex County. Full of rolling hills, mountains, packed trout streams and bucolic lakes. It even bragged some surviving timid black bears that penis-challenged hunters had failed to eradicate in their perpetual attempt to prove their manhood by putting food out for them in the woods, waiting in trees with their weapons, then shot-gunning them down, cubs and all.

Hardly convenient, the wealthy found the remoteness objectionable, leaving no albatrosses for the government to tear down. The lack of access to mass transit, actually the reason the area had stayed rural, undesirable to the masses for the same reason.

An hour before dinner, Scotty's parents started fighting again; the same old thing. His mother, one of the four million polio victims in the United States from the epidemic of 2018, had frequently yet unsuccessfully tried to convince his father to relocate. She dreamed about better healthcare and quality of life in a less populated area. Like Sussex County.

His big sister, Abby, a dialysis patient, needed to get to the hospital three times a week. As a toddler, she'd developed chronic kidney disease, acute and undoubtedly fatal, requiring her to be in and out of hospital since a baby. She really needed a kidney transplant, but they didn't have the money to buy one from China or South America like the other patients of loftier financial means.

When the country decided to worship at the altar of socialized medicine, an understandably desperate shortage of doctors ensued. Over-utilized emergency rooms, with a standard back up of thirty six hours on any normal day before the polio epidemic, suddenly morphed into requiring an appointment to get in. Dying before your appointment became common, creating a huge underground market which sold these appointments to the highest bidder. Family allowances limited the amount of doctor visits per year. Inevitably, rationing became as necessary as breathing.

Simple sore throats or innocuous coughs, easily overlooked by busy adults trying to avoid burning a valuable medical visit, still spread germs. Unfortunately, polio was highly contagious. An airline passenger can infect an entire plane with one phlegmy throat. The government burden of bloated bureaucracy put the final nail in that coffin.

The epidemic started because of a Muslim law, passed in 2005, in Northern Nigeria. They issued an Islamic Fatwa, declaring the polio vaccine part of a secret conspiracy by the United States and the United Nations against the Muslim faith. Their claim declared that the vaccine drops, secretly designed to sterilize the Muslim true believers, stimulated the virus. It then reappeared in Nigeria and spread throughout Africa. In this world of high-speed airline transportation it didn't take long to span the globe. Legal immigration figures show the number one source of immigrants in the good ol' U.S.A. to be from Africa. And who could blame them?

The SNW Party now exercised iron control over the government. The exceptionality of The United States had started its decline long ago when the masses realized they could use their vote to elect officials willing to rape the country in their efforts to buy those very votes. So they elected the politician and party that promised them the most swag. They didn't care that someone must inevitably pay for it, so long as it wasn't them.

As a result, availability of capital to grow the private sector diminished. Small businesses suffered and disappeared. Taxes shot through the roof. Large corporations left the country along with the wealthy. The Hollywood elite bailed quickly; France, London and Mexico their preferred destinations. A pound of chopped meat in a grocery store (if you could find it on the shelf) now cost $33.00. And it was mostly pink slime fillers at that. Thank heavens for food stamps.

The country now consisted of a populous that couldn't catch a break as rival political parties outdid themselves robbing from the taxpayers. The country, no longer a melting pot, became a nation of fighting tribal factions and competing ideologies. The SNW Party, the Muslim Brotherhood, the Green and the smaller Republican Party perpetually slandered each other in their quest to control what remained of the country while the people did their best to hold their families together.

There no longer existed a national language. Children attended school for four hours a day, eight months a year; the average work week a mere twenty five hours. The public insisted that politicians respected their need for rest and recreation. If they didn't, they lost their jobs—voted out. Capitalism reigned no longer.

The outdated pieces of paper called the Constitution lost their relevance and respect. The new law of the land required the courts to consider the beliefs and requirements of all global groups when assessing legal responsibility. Political correctness ran amok. And the deficit—stratospheric. Why do you think China had such a large economic presence? They owned the United States. Yes, what a lovely country the people lived in.

The Chinese depended on that. Money for research and development in the U.S. had vanished. Our scientists had moved to other countries as did the best doctors, the rich, Wall Street and the entrepreneurs who had found their spirits crushed by taxes and burdensome regulations. Everyone needed capital to survive. There was no capital in the U. S. The government would spend, spend and spend on entitlements and kickbacks to their donor cronies. It didn't matter who was in power—they *all* did it and there was no way to stop it. A ruling class of vampires that threw a few trinkets to the people to keep them quiet and willing to hold out their arms to have their blood sucked. Surprisingly, the world's super powers, China, Russia and Iran still allowed the U.S. to borrow money, even though repayment of the principal appeared unlikely. And the interest sure was a doozey.

And then the polio came; the U.S the hardest hit. Over ten million children and four million adults died in the U. S. The highest percentage of adults came from minority communities, mostly immigrants from third world countries. Another three million left maimed and crippled to one degree or another. Urgent medical care meant emergency rooms came under siege; the doctors, almost nonexistent. Too many hospitals closed for lack of operating funds; too little reimbursement.

It didn't come as a surprise to many to learn the United States Health and Human Services Department had quietly stopped budgeting for the creation and implementation of the polio vaccine in 2013. They had taken responsibility for vaccines and immunizations away from parents who had long ago rejected the poisons in the makeup of the vaccines. The boards of education, no longer monitoring the children's vaccination requirements, demanded congressional investigations that went nowhere. Conspiracy advocates abounded. The most popular theory postulated that the virus, deliberately released by the government, would serve to thin the ranks of the entitlement classes. Abdicating responsibility to deadly disease; clearly far easier and more expedient than Congress risking re-election in a controversial attempt at fiscal responsibility. C'est la vie. Massive riots in the streets enabled citizens to vent, but the efforts for change advanced anemically.

Scotty grew hungry for his dinner while waiting for Germaine. If his best buddy didn't show soon, they might lose their prize to the big kids. He didn't want the big kids to spot him without Germaine for backup. The last time that had happened, they had held him down and pulled off his pants. They had jeered and taunted him, calling him Scotty-Watty Tissue Paper and worse yet, Ass-Wipe. They left him pantless on the pavement to slink home in disgrace. His mommy had held him and shed tears with him. His daddy had made fun of him and called him a sissy boy. He didn't think sissy boy sounded nice coming from his daddy's mouth. Now his daddy referred to both him and his big sister as parasites.

He'd smiled the first time he'd heard it. It had sounded like a big important word. He'd loved the way it rolled off his tongue and liked to repeat the word over and over, enjoying the syllables that popped out of his mouth so satisfyingly. Then he noticed his mother's face after his father had said it. It looked crumpled in. That's when he realized it was a bad word. Now, the word just slithered out of his mouth like a venomous snake looking for prey to strike.

He developed trouble sleeping, nightmares a common occurrence. He never remembered any of his dreams, but he knew they always contained a big dark murky figure that resembled his dad. Unfortunately, Scotty had developed into a suspicious, defensive little boy, trusting only his mother and sister.

He loved his half-sister, Abby. Abby's daddy and his mom had never married. Everyone said young and foolish made a bad combination for marriage. That's what Abby said, too. He didn't think his mom had ever behaved foolishly. If she'd been his age, he would have made her his very best friend. Even though playing with a girl made you look like a loser.

Thirteen year old Abby became Scotty's strongest advocate. Whenever Scotty refused to go outside for fear of bodily harm, Abby would sit him down and spin stories of imaginary worlds, fantastic creatures and handsome, brave little boys. He loved hearing Abby's stories even more than playing with Germaine.

That's why he couldn't understand why his daddy ignored Abby. His mommy said sisters and brothers must always protect one another. But he knew his daddy didn't want to protect Abby.

Late one night when he got up to go potty, he heard his parents fighting. He heard his father shout something about Abby hanging around his neck like an anchor. He heard his daddy call Abby a bad name. His daddy said he didn't want to be responsible for a bastard kid that didn't belong to him.

Overhearing his daddy gave him a stomachache. His troubled sleep left him tired and cranky the next morning. But he still managed to promise his mommy he would always protect Abby, even if he'd to stand on a chair to do it. He thought it would make his mother happy. He didn't understand why she cried instead.

Late one fall day, Scotty came home from grade school, his paperwork in his eager hands. He wanted to show his mom the smiley face the teacher had given him. His daddy was supposed to take Abby to the hospital for her weekly dialysis treatment. Mommy worked six days a week at the grocery store, so Daddy reluctantly took responsibility. When Scotty remarked that Daddy should work so Mommy could stay home more, he claimed he'd very important things to do and that a dummy like Scotty wouldn't understand. Mommy looked like her tummy hurt when Daddy said things like that.

Actually, the little boy didn't recall his daddy ever working like Mommy did. He often saw her late at night, removing her shiny leg brace to massage her tired muscles.

Scotty realized most of the dads in his building didn't work. They formulated important matters to discuss in the rec room. The dads wouldn't let little kids in the rec room because of the beer and smoking. So when he found Abby unconscious on the floor of her bedroom, he ran down to the basement and pounded on the locked rec room door.

"Hello, anyone in there? Daddy, I need you. Daddy, Daddy. Help." He knew Abby should have gone to the hospital this morning. Why hadn't Daddy taken her? But no one would open the door to a crying six year old. He tried again, banging over and over. The door suddenly opened, omitting smoke and loud raucous music.

"Kid, what cha doing screaming out here? Get lost." The big man wore an old stained shirt, the sleeves rolled up over his fat hairy arms. He exuded an unfamiliar bad smell.

"Is my daddy here? I need him to come home; Abby's on the floor." Scotty danced nervously, his voice small and frightened, his wandering eye floating erratically.

"I'm not gonna say it again. Don't be bangin' on this door." The big man burped, sending a gust of rancid beer breath in Scotty's face. He cringed, the door slamming in his face.

Scotty knew saving Abby by himself would require some bravery.

He ran outside into the dirty street, his heart pounding so hard he thought the bullies in the neighborhood might hear him.

Choking back his sobs, he ran up and down the street, dodging cars and screaming for the police. He glimpsed the old grannies from the neighborhood who congregated at the corner, lounging in cheap plastic chairs, holding court on the sidewalks. He scrambled out of the street, hurrying toward them.

"Abby's going to die. She's on the floor. Please, we need help."

Unable to hold back the tears overflowing his wild eyes, he dragged the grannies to his family's apartment. A nice Muslim lady sat with him while two other black grannies made a few cellphone calls.

Soon, three strapping black men entered the apartment. Scotty, positive they would rob the apartment, stuck to them like glue. Relieved, he watched them lift Abby in their arms and carry her out of the apartment. He tried to follow.

"Hey kiddo, you stay here until your mom comes home. Your sister's very sick. You need to hold down the fort. This nice lady will stay with you." One of the black men, his eyes soft and moist, ran his hand along Scotty's shoulder giving him a reassuring stroke and softly shut the door behind him.

The nice Muslim lady stayed with him until his mommy came home from work. He hoped Abby didn't die. Fear made him pray.

He didn't know much about what happened after that. His mommy asked him to stay in his room. He heard lots of crying and silences. Then his daddy came home and the screaming started. He didn't know what it meant, but he felt terror-stricken anyway. He began to relax when the cops took his daddy away. Abby came home a week later, alive but painfully thin. Scotty began to sleep much, much better.

A few days later, his mother silently handed him a cardboard box, telling him to pack his toys. She folded all their clothes except for Daddy's, the brace on her afflicted leg clanking around the apartment as she packed up their little lives.

The night before the move, his mother sat them both down for a talk.

"Scotty, do you understand we're moving far away?" She pulled her light brown hair back in a ponytail; long wisps escaping to frame her thin stressed face, her voice low and tired.

"Yes, Mommy," he assured his mother, not understanding the

meaning of far away. But he loved and trusted his mom. He knew every line on her wonderful face. A smile failed to appear as he scrutinized her expression. Somehow, he realized, she needed him to be okay with the move.

Abby picked him up and sat him on her lap.

"Honey, you shouldn't strain yourself like that. The nurse said—"

"Mom, it's okay. Let me help." She rocked Scotty on her lap. Her pretty face lit up, her affection for Scotty giving him confidence as he looked into her eyes, laughing. "You're our big guy aren't you, Scotty? It's going to be you, me and Mom. What a great team. We can do anything, right?"

"Right." Shouting and laughing, he looked at his mom. "Right, Mommy?"

"Right, baby, a great team." She finally joined in the laughter, her children's optimism infectious.

Chapter 2

The scary move to Sussex County brought about many changes; not the least of which was Scotty never again seeing his only playmate, Germaine. Germaine said he would beg his mom to bring him for a visit, but Germaine didn't have a daddy to drive him there.

Luckily, Abby recovered from her sickness. Her physician assistant (she never actually saw a doctor, ever, not in her whole life) determined her kidney would have no lasting damage. Maybe. From now on, they must watch very carefully to make sure Abby got to her dialysis on time. It was critical. Mom told them about the cute little neighborhood not far from their new home that offered a health clinic with the services Abby needed. Relief washed over Scotty. He didn't want to have to save Abby again. The traumatic event reverberated in his memory, too much for a six-year-old boy.

Their sad, little three-bedroomed ranch in Sussex County looked as lonely and forlorn as Scotty felt. The roof desperately needed repairs. When it rained, they ran around, laughing and bumping into one another with pots in their hands, collecting the drips. When they took showers, the water didn't stay hot for long; the last one in froze. They learned they must accept the landlord's response to their complaints. He gave them two choices, suck it up or get out.

They did their best to make it a home, and Mrs. Preston made sure she kept it spotless and full of love. Scotty screamed with happiness, thrilled to find it included a tiny backyard with his very own tree. The air smelled clean and fragrant. But, best of all, it didn't have his daddy. His nightmares stopped. Whenever his mother mentioned he could visit his dad, his heart raced with panic. On those occasions, he usually pottied in his bed while he slept. The next day, when his mommy changed his bed, he would tell her all about his nightmare. Her face slipped into such a haggard and defeated bearing that he felt swamped with guilt, convinced his father's pronouncements about him might come true.

Sadly, the little boy found no playmates in his hilly little neighborhood. The homes were mostly occupied by black and Spanish families, along with the usual separate enclave of Muslims. The children in the neighborhood took one look at his bald spots and disfiguring scars, and refused to play with him, turning up their noses. They made fun of his wandering eye, calling him cootie head, dick wad, faggot and douche bag. The older boys would jeer at him, enjoying his hurt. The most aggressive pushed him to the ground, kicking dirt and gravel at him to cover his cootie bugs.

Scotty wandered around and around the neighborhood, looking for someone to play with. His loneliness made him long to grow up quickly. Then he could do anything he wanted, not needing the attention or approval of kids who felt it necessary to call him ass wipe. His memories tasted nasty, festering like an infected wound.

One day, he found the top of the hill behind his neighborhood. He discovered a curious path that tempted him into the woods. The dead leaves from tall, thick grandfather oaks, dried and crinkled, disintegrated underfoot as he explored. Over time, he learned to entertain himself in the woods, fighting imaginary wars with imaginary magical creatures. The woods became an enchanting place for him. He felt peace. He felt safe. He loved the small clearings drizzled with dappled sunlight, the occasional sighting of little creatures. He never felt lonely, seduced by the magic of timid rabbits, quarreling squirrels, hyperactive chipmunks and the silent family of deer; all his unwitting playmates, enchanting him with their innocence and acceptance.

Today he turned seven. He looked forward to the scrumptious cake his mother always baked for his birthday. He knew Abby planned to have a special gift for him from the meager money she earned from the Muslim family she babysat for. He could hardly contain his excitement during the school day, which passed too slowly. He thought he would age another year while he waited. The usual snubs from his classmates mattered not, his mind focused on the happy party waiting for him at home.

Running up to his now familiar door after the school bus dropped him off, he jerked in surprise, seeing his father's car in the drive, hearing shouts and angry voices.

Letting himself in, he trembled at the sight of his father. His heartbeat ratcheted up, thumping hard as his breathing came fast and shallow, his stomach starting a slow roil. He witnessed his father's arms looped around his mother's neck as he tried to force her to kiss him. She fought back, trying to slip out of his grip with little success, her balance a hindrance because of her brace.

His father's expression hardened; angry and ugly. A sneer deformed his thin lips as he slowly strangled her while Scotty beat on his father's legs, vainly trying to protect his mother. She screamed, fighting him off until a desperate shove sent her falling back on the kitchen table where Scotty's birthday cake sat, waiting to have the candles lit for his party. Seven beautiful blue candles on top of rich chocolate icing. His mom caught her balance on the kitchen table, sending his beautiful birthday cake flying.

Everyone froze as the cake landed upside down, splattering on the hardwood floor. Staring at his ruined birthday cake, Scotty felt his stomach turn inside out, queasiness ready to explode. And a little something new: anger. The kind of anger that festers and simmers beneath the surface, cooking in its own poison while it twists the mind with bitterness. Picking up the remains of the cake, he threw it at his father who just laughed at him, calling him a crybaby and a little turd.

"I'm not a little turd."

Sobbing, he ran out the door, up the hill and into the woods. He just kept running, past all his favorite spots, into the deep woods, his sobs turning to anger, magnified by the resentment of his afflictions.

Slowing down, he dropped to the ground, leaning up against a hillside unfamiliar to him. He tried to block the memory of his daddy's belittling taunting tone and the damaged look on his mom's face. Restlessly, he wandered along the hillside until he turned a corner, stepping back in surprise.

Before him stood a massive granite boulder. He eyeballed the massive rock, wondering how he dare claim it for his own. He noticed handholds, seemingly carved into the side of the rock. *Hmm, can I pull myself up?* Approaching the rock, he struggled with the handholds, finally reaching the top. *What a great spot for a fort.* Curling up in a depression, he felt the warmth from the sun seep from the rock into his body. His drowsy eyes slowly closed over his tear-stained cheeks and he drifted off into an uneasy sleep.

The creature roused herself from a deep slumber, feeling the presence of a large life form. She sensed its closeness, but noted it was not yet in the deep quiet cavern of the Hive. She called the Hive home, her safety well assured for over a century. Sadly, she coped with constant loneliness; her only companions the occasional woodland creature that found its way into the cavern. Periodically, she would venture out to observe the behavior of the human creatures of this planet, caution an imperative.

The trauma witnessed over a century ago still smoldered sharply in her mind; the guilt, just as fresh. She could have intervened when she became suspicious of her birth Brother's mental and physical damage during her emergence.

Or perhaps it had happened during the Womb's entry into the Earth's atmosphere. Maybe the Womb had failed to properly care for Brother, although it had certainly cared for her without complaint. She often suspected the Womb had deliberately allowed the incident to escalate just so it could study the outcome. How else could the Womb learn how to interpret the actions of the humans?

She agreed they merited study, but her sensibilities had cringed as the slaughter had transpired. Most of the time, the Womb took a hands-off policy, not wanting to interfere with the culture of any species, unless the species became catastrophically aggressive to others, of course. But this was a minion, the Womb's chosen.

She remembered back a full century to the time she'd last laid eyes on the doomed Sister. She'd considered making contact without her Brother's knowledge when the Sister had suddenly appeared one day at the rock that disguised the entrance to the cavern.

She'd watched from her hidden position in the forest as the Sister had first discovered her birth Brother and carried him away from the Hive. She didn't understand why Brother hadn't objected. Confusion ruled as she'd tried to puzzle out why her birth Brother had neglected to begin his mission. Instead, he'd involved himself intimately in the Sister's life, apparently satisfied with the tiny part of his mission that he did manage to accomplish: creating two new Elders to assist him.

As it had turned out, an evil human Brother stalked the Sister. He'd captured her and participated in a brutal murder. She knew how bloodthirsty the evil species behaved on this planet, observing firsthand what had happened to the Sister, her birth Brother and his own little furry pet from the safety of the hilltop near the forest edge. She remembered with pain her birth Brother's golden life force splashing on the unyielding ground. She bitterly remembered the look of astonishment then disgust as the evil Brother that had murdered him wiped the sacred life force off the heels of his boots.

The shock had numbed her as the mesmerizing golden light and vital thought projections had faded from Brother's disfigured eyes. She'd actually felt the genetic mental connection shared by all of her species being brutally severed. Running back through the woods, she'd vowed to never leave the Hive until she could assure her own safety.

It was incomprehensible to believe the bloodthirsty human Brothers would reject the very gifts meant to rescue them and justify the complex energy expended long ago on their behalf. But they had; making the unfortunate choice that had pronounced their death sentence. She wondered if the humans had rejected Sister's new tail. The humans must realize by now that a tail was nothing new to their species. The success of the mission had demanded complex alterations of their physical and biological systems. It was a good thing that only the tail had manifested, not the antlers. That would have been a disaster.

Determination coursed through her solar veins. Her job rested on her ability to ensure the Elder's grand plan, offering salvation for both species, not failure. Success would ensure the redemption from the Womb that minions had sought for hundreds of thousands of years. Perhaps the humans needed a different type of manifestation. She would have to ponder. If she could alter a few of her own cells and enzymes, a solution might be available. Maybe the Womb would help her. But her intention would never include getting rid of her own beautiful tail. The engineering for that would be too complex to attempt without help. She felt comforted by her tail; even as she knew it had a life of its own.

She curiously wondered why her Brother hadn't tried to contact her. She'd have been willing to complete the mission in his stead. As things stood, now that Brother had expired, her honor (and genetic programming) obligated her to eventually complete the mission for him anyway.

But she remained hesitant. Over the last century she'd observed the savage violence that this species perpetrated on itself. She understood why the Womb authorized the mission. And, just like the Womb, she now saw little reason to save this species. She suspected the Elders truly had made a tragic mistake. They had offered excuse after excuse for this life form, hoping evolution would tame them. Then, with influence from the Elders no longer a factor, the Womb had passed judgment, ordering the mission. But the possibility existed that her decision might abet an error. She decided to take her time. This planet needed much more observation; direct observation. She hoped the Womb would allow her the time. Maybe if she could just find *The One*.

It would truly be a tragedy if she decided to let this species self-destruct, along with Brother's newly obtained Elder state—now tragically lost. What a surprising discovery that had been. Her species had said goodbye to Elders long ago. In anger at their hubris, the Womb had altered the minions' ability to become Elders after discovering their fateful mistake, forever preventing healing of humans, but not other life forms. Now, minion expiration came through old age or the birth process. It appeared that, for some reason, Brother's own genetic instructions, meant to prevent the conversion, had failed. She could not know for sure without a laboratory at her disposal. Her mind, distracted by the biology, pondered the complexity of their enzymes.

She wondered if she could achieve that lofty state of Elder herself. Had she already? She'd easily surpassed her normal life span long ago. She'd never know until the first opportunity to heal a Brother or Sister presented itself. Yet she refused to try until she decided that this species deserved it. As of yet, her doubts remained strong.

She could stay in the Hive as long as it took, but she was in doubt as to the amount of time the Womb would allow her. She wanted to wait until she'd received a sign of worthiness. But she was terribly lonely. Her species thrived on close contact. They lived in communal groups—hives. Similar to what were called families here on Earth, only much larger. She'd noticed that most of the other species of this planet also lived in families. Of course, she'd expected human life on this planet to have evolved similar habits. Sighing, she worried about the damage perpetual isolation would do to her mental state.

The Hive, under supervision of the Womb, would always take care of all the needs a carbon based life form required to survive; irrespective of their metabolism. The Womb, being indestructible, easily accomplished all tasks in the pursuit of creating life. But she remained alone, unable to stop the toll her isolation undeniably looked to extract. Surely her own iridescent eyes dimmed. Maybe the time to do something about her dilemma neared.

The creature planned to take an excursion to the surface sometime soon. She needed to check on the various groups that clustered in the small buildings on land that had previously grown stunning fruit orchards.

Her monumental shock when she'd witnessed the fruit trees ripped from the earth, destroying a unique gift given to the humans, shook her to her core. Gone the orchards that would feed so many, for so long. Within a decade, the miracle seeds from those trees and the crops would have spread naturally all over the world, feeding everyone. The wanton waste was unforgivable. As a result, the

Womb angrily intensified its plan for revenge. This species clearly refused to learn. How they'd become programmed for self-destruction, she didn't know. Perhaps if the Elders had acquiesced differently to the Womb after the discovery of their forbidden experiment, they could have intervened, guiding evolution to a more satisfactory outcome—the very guidance that the Womb had enjoyed exerting everywhere else, feeling no planet too insignificant. But the Womb had forbidden the guidance. The humans were on their own, a punishment they were unaware of.

The creature disconnected from the Hive wall, her tail dry as it withdrew from the thick membrane. Leaving her private chamber, she shuffled and bobbed her way up the long lonely trail to the outside world.

Arriving at the end of the underground trail, the creature reached her hand into the cavern wall, asking it to part. When the wall split, she squeezed and contorted her way around the rocks and boulders blocking and disguising the Hive. Glancing back, she made sure the Hive closed behind her.

She remembered that the blame for the catastrophic events of a century ago belonged partially to her. After her Emergence, she'd left her Brother behind in his helpless hibernation state in her zeal to explore topside. If her Emergence had occurred back on Oolaha, surrounded by all the help her Brother had needed to emerge from hibernation and begin transition, his eventual expiration would have been successful. She herself would have received proper guidance, allowing the time for her awareness to digest all the stimuli being transmitted to her mind from her own transcription cells. She wouldn't have run off halfcocked and uninformed, failing to ensure the Hive closed behind her, making the fatal mistake that had allowed the Sister to enter and discover her birth Brother.

Having reached maturity, she realized her birth Brother must have called the human to use for his own recovery, but she doubted her Brother's powers had been strong enough.

The Womb created the energy she and Brother needed to survive as a by-product of its slow feeding on the organic material it rested on. It was an inexhaustible source of the energy she needed to feed on as long as she remained underground. Once above ground, she took all she needed from the sun. She could also use a human Brother or Sister, but she strongly intended to stay far away for now. Besides, she much preferred the slower absorption from the sun. It reacted more efficiently with her metabolism. Taking nourishment from a human left her species confused and disoriented. Perhaps the very reason Brother had left the Hive with the Sister. Maybe confusion had reigned.

The occasional animal that wandered near could obviously smell the membrane and knew the Womb lived. They usually entered out of curiosity and perhaps hunger, causing little damage. But she knew the Sister had entered because of her own carelessness.

Not only did she carry overwhelming guilt and barely tolerable loneliness, but she knew her species probably didn't know she existed. They monitored the energy outflow from the Womb membrane to determine if Brother still lived, but the Womb couldn't make a distinction between its minions. They undoubtedly thought she was Brother. The Womb had never registered any simultaneous energy draws, cluing them into her existence back home. Over the last century, they'd recorded her withdrawal, mistakenly believing it to be that of Brother's.

At some point, Brother would have died. They wouldn't know that he'd an offspring or that he'd become an Elder. They'd expect the humans to carry out the mission of their own volition after her Brother's death. Monitoring this planet would provide few answers. Only an Elder could communicate through the Womb to Oolaha. But the Womb knew. That's all that really mattered. Oh well, she could only do her best. When she thought the humans were ready, she'd begin.

Pushing all the unanswerable questions from her rambling mind, she stepped around the cairn of rocks that helped protect the Hive and stretched up to the sun. Sensing the life form she'd detected earlier, she peered around the rocks, unable to locate it. She decided she'd scramble up her favorite rock to get closer to the sun where she'd be unobserved. She loved to curl up in the depression at the top. It soaked up the sun and warmed her fat belly when she nestled in.

Reaching out with her long slender fingers, she touched the rock. Her suction-like pads helped pull her body up as she climbed, creeping up the side of the rock. Her head swiveled up and down as she gauged the distance from the top to the bottom. Pulling herself up and over the top, she made an unexpected discovery. There, in her depression, lay the life form: a small human Brother. He wore the coverings humans liked to swaddle themselves in, measuring almost twice her size, yet appearing harmless enough as he slept. Quivering with anticipation, she decided to quietly sit and watch, wrapping her golden tail around herself.

As she observed, she weighed the attraction her birth Brother had felt for his human Sister. She longed to reach out and touch the long fibers on the young Brother's head, very different from the fuzz and fur on her own body. She wondered if it felt softer. It certainly didn't keep him warm in the way her pelt did. She guessed that explained the swaddling. They wouldn't be so vulnerable to heat fluctuations if their metabolisms had evolved closer to that of her species; so much simpler. She sniffed, knowing that if she was consulted on the design she'd certainly make improvements. Her puzzled eyes drifted over the strange markings on his head and the scars on his skin, shaking her head at his obvious signs of disease; the poor human Brother.

It was no wonder the Womb had decided they must be revisited for intervention. Perhaps the time should have come much sooner, before they'd started to live inside caves instead of out in the open like herds. Before they'd learned to practice wanton bloodlust, employed so often for reasons other than survival. They were a lost cause. Banishing all her troubling thoughts, she concentrated on the little Brother. Without realizing what she was doing, she let her probing aura coalesce in his mind. And, suddenly, his eyes flew open.

Chapter 3

What the—? Scrambling quickly up on his butt, Scotty scooted out of the depression, edging to the back of the rock. There he sat and stared at the funny looking creature, eh no, elf. No, fairy. Yeah, it must be a fairy. Wow. He'd found an actual golden fairy. Hopping up, he made a grab for it. The fairy unwound his long tail and disappeared over the side of the rock. Scotty leaned over the edge, the fairy nowhere to be seen.

Carefully, he lowered himself down the rock, slipping on the sharp footholds as he descended. Desperately, he looked around, trying to discover where the fairy had disappeared to. *Gee, Mom will never believe this.* He wasn't sure he could convince her unless he brought the fairy home. *Holy mackerel, no one will believe this.* Excitement gripped him; a touch of something special in his life for the first time.

He knew he must find the hiding place where the fairy lived. Stumbling over the loose pile of rock heaped near the hillside, he discovered an enormous rip in his pant leg. Squatting down, he examined it. *Mom won't be happy about this.* And he didn't even have the fairy to show her. Straightening up, something caught his eye. A golden glint, just like the fairy.

He tripped over the rocks, his footing unsteady until he located the place the glint came from. Digging down between the rocks, his fingers withdrew an object. A coin. He rubbed it on his jeans, removing some of the crusted dirt so deeply embedded. He stared, his wandering eye refusing to focus.

Turning it around and over in his little fingers, the heavy coin finally revealed more of the golden sheen and a date, 1702. Hmm, it wasn't even new. He wondered if the fairy had left it for him.

Maybe the fairy knew of his birthday and had left it as a gift to make up for his dad ruining his day, hurting his mom and calling him bad names. If it did, Scotty wished the fairy could have made the coin a new shiny one. But at least he could show some kind of proof to his mom now. Glancing around for the last time, he brushed off his pants and started home.

The creature stood on the inside of the Hive. She felt full of furious agitation, yet oddly exhilarated. She wished the little Brother hadn't run off. She supposed she could have followed him. She wondered if he might return. If he did, she should figure out a better way to handle the situation. Even though the encounter had gone badly, she felt different; hopeful. She wasn't sure why, but she had a feeling about this little human Brother. Maybe he could be *The One*.

The little boy hurried down the path that took him out of his magical woods, the golden coin tucked safely in his pocket. Running down the hill past his neighbors' homes, he could see his house. He noted with relief that his father's car no longer sat in the driveway. Bursting breathlessly through the front door, he beheld his mom and Abby waiting for him.

"Oh baby, we were so worried. Where did you go? We called and called. Didn't you hear us? We even went up to the woods." His frazzled mom hurried over as fast as she could, her brace clinking at her side. She sat awkwardly on the floor in front of him, holding out her arms to sweep him to her chest. Tears coursed down her face, the worry lines standing out in relief as she softly ran her fingers over the bald spots on his head.

"It's okay, Mom. I'm okay. Please don't cry, I'm sorry I ran away." He hugged her tight, his young head fitting under her neck for comfort.

"Hi, sport," Abby said. "Glad you came home—got'cha something." Joining her brother and mom on the floor, she gave Scotty a kiss and put a brightly wrapped slender gift in his lap. He fingered the ribbon with wonder. The bow was bright gold. Unwrapping the gift, he grinned in amazement at the book about fairies. *Wow, did this mean they knew?* Leafing through the book, he located a whole chapter on wood fairies. He would study that chapter first. He knew he'd learn everything he needed to know about his fairy in the book.

"Gee, thanks, Ab. Mom, I met a fairy in the woods today. He left me a present. Did you tell him it was my birthday?" His face shined with unconcealed innocence.

"Sweetie, I'm sure you met your very own birthday fairy. But what do you mean, he gave you a present?"

Scotty sighed, knowing his mom worried about child molesters. Though it was unlikely any lived in the neighborhood, she monitored everything, knowing they had to be extra careful ever since they'd abolished the sexual predator register (declared unconstitutional—they have rights, you know).

"Mom, he did leave me a present. He's a golden fairy. Abby, do fairies usually have a tail? His tail glowed. And he left me this." Pulling out the coin from his pocket, he proudly held it up for his sister and mom. Taking it from him to examine, his mother carefully scrutinized the coin.

"This coin is very old sweetie, old is good. That's what makes it valuable."

"Is it a special coin, Mom? It must be special because I got it from the golden fairy and he knew about my birthday." Scotty's chest inflated, his wandering eye unexpectedly centered in his eyeball.

Looking over to the kitchen table, a new birthday cake winked at him. He could tell his mom had purchased it at the bakery. He wondered where she'd got the money from, but the moment contained so much joy he pushed away his guilt. Jumping up, he tugged on both of them.

"Mom, let's have cake. I want to blow out my candles and make a wish." Hurrying over to the table, she lit the candles as she sang to him. While they blazed with flame, he made a wish and blew them all out. Smiling happily to himself, he realized that, this time, his birthday wish would come true, absolutely convinced his golden fairy would grant it. He couldn't wait to wake up the next morning to hear of his father's death.

When bedtime came, his mother tucked him in. Noticing his gold coin and his new book in bed with him, she removed them, placing both on his dresser.

"Sweetie, I think we'll put your coin someplace safe, it's probably very valuable. I'll look into it and see what I can find out. Good night, birthday boy." As his mother shut off the light, the last thoughts filling his head swam with images of the fairy and the most fantastic birthday ever. Scotty slumbered fitfully, unaware of the probing flashes of residual rainbow light that sent fingers to tumble around in his brain.

Going off to school the next morning, he took his new book with him. Reading the chapter on wood fairies, he found no mention of golden ones with long glowing tails. As a matter of fact, he didn't see any fairies with tails. They all wore wings of some kind. Certainly none of them with horns like his golden fairy. His disappointment acute, excitement dimmed, he slowly grasped that he might be wrong about his fairy. No, he knew a fairy when he saw one. What else could it have been?

Riding home on the school bus, his spirits flagged, disappointed to find the rain pouring down. He wanted to return to the big rock and wait for the fairy, afraid that if he didn't show up, the fairy might give up on him and find a new little boy to spend time with. His mom waited for him at the bus stop. Taking her hand, he scooted under her umbrella. Smiling gently, she smoothed back the wisps of hair that refused to cover his ringworm scars no matter how she brushed them.

"Honey, your father called. He'd like to visit this weekend and apologize for his behavior. Would you like to see him?"

"No, no!" Scotty screamed, his face turning white. His father was still alive? The fairy hadn't come through for him. Something had gone wrong with his wish. Maybe he needed to tell it directly to the fairy.

"Mommy, I need to go to the woods today." His voice frantic, he begged for her permission.

"Don't be silly. You'll get soaked. You're not going anywhere except home with me, silly." Arriving at their front door, she closed the umbrella and scooted him into the house.

Hanging up his jacket, he ran to Abby's bedroom where he found her studying. She was in high school now, her time no longer as available to him. He climbed up on to her bed, trying to fit in her lap the way he used to as a tot.

"Come on, little dude, I need to get my homework done." Abby laughingly rained kisses down on his sad face, signs of his infant impetigo less of a beacon now that a growth spurt looked to be in play. Stroking his patchy fine hair back from his face, she pushed her books aside, cuddling up with her brother on her pillows. "What's wrong, Scotty?"

Tears slowly leaked down his chubby cheeks as he snuggled up to his sister. "Abby, I love you."

"I love you too, champ. What's going on?"

He put his ear up to his sister's to whisper. "I think daddy's going to move back in with us." He quickly looked to his sister's face to gauge her reaction. Abby looked grim, but she hugged him tightly.

"No, Scotty; that will never happen. Mom promised he would never get the chance to hurt her or demean us again. So put a smile on your face and get ready for dinner."

"Okay, but if he does, I'm going to make a magic sword to protect us with. I'll always protect you and Mommy." Scrambling off Abby's bed, he ran to his own room. He took out his book of fairies from his backpack and slid it into a drawer. He would solve his fairy dilemma on his own and in secrecy. That's probably what his fairy wanted anyway.

Sitting down to dinner, he noticed his mom serving mac and cheese again, on the fancy blue and white plastic plates she'd got as a wedding gift before his birth. The aroma of hot gooey cheese tantalized him. Mom made it almost every other day because he loved it, naturally. Chowing down, he noticed Abby and mommy talking in low voices about the welfare money. They needed the welfare money. Everyone got welfare money.

"Kids, I have some important news for you." He looked closer at his mom's face, her lips tightly pursed, her eyes tense. Not with anger, more like scary disappointment. Did he see fear on his mom's face? *What's going on?* Looking at Abby, he could tell she already knew.

"We're going to have some new house guests."

"No, not Daddy, please." His stomach started to ache. His mommy reached over to stroke his arm, calming him.

"No baby, it won't be your father. He's gone for good. I don't even know where he's going, but I do know he'll leave New Jersey. We're going to share the house and expenses with another family. It's all arranged. You know the Diaz family, doesn't Jose go to your school, Abby?"

"Yes, Mom, he does, he's okay. Is the whole family coming?"

"Yes, except for Mr. Diaz. He'll be heading to Mexico to try to jump the fence. If he's successful, he stands a good chance of nabbing a job, and they'll probably move out if that happens. If he gets caught, he'll go to prison. It's a felony in Mexico; they're very serious about protecting jobs for their own people. Then we'll have to think about a more permanent solution."

"Solution to what, Mom?" Abby asked.

"Honey, anyone with a job is being removed from the welfare rolls. We can keep our housing stipend and our energy assistance, thank God. And the food stamps will help until they cut them out. My paycheck won't cover the rest of our expenses. Not with the co-pays for Abby's dialysis. The Diaz family is losing their welfare check, too.

"But, Mom—why? Why is the check going to stop? Can we talk to the mailman? Is this the week he comes, or is it next week?" Scotty's voice faltered with fright.

"Don't worry, honey, everything will work out if we all pull together. The government is just finding it difficult to collect the money from the rich people. They can't give it to us unless they collect it first. I know it's not fair, the rich have so much compared to us. It's not the government's fault. The rich people are just getting better at hiding the money. We'll learn to make do. That's why the Diaz family is moving in.

"All the boys will sleep together in your room, Scotty. The three of us will sleep together in Abby's room. I'm going to move my bed in there. The Diaz family will have two rooms for six people. Most importantly, they'll pay us rent. That'll make up for most of the loss of the welfare." Grinning, his mom tried to put a smile on her face, but Scotty could see the struggle.

"Mom, as long as we're together, that's all that matters." Abby got up and put her arms around her mother. "Hey, champ, since we're going to be roomies, why don't we do the dishes and give Mom a break?"

Scotty understood that many changes loomed large in his life. As he cleared the table, he thought about Jose Diaz, the only one in the family he recognized. Jose, an older kid on his bus a couple of years ago, didn't speak English very well. He kept to himself, never horsing around with the other kids, although he'd nodded now and then as Scotty boarded the bus. Rumors said he'd grown up in another country.

Helping his mother up from her chair, he glanced out the window, hoping the sun had finished chasing away the rain. The thunderclouds covered most of the sun as it began its nightly disappearance below the horizon. Oh well, maybe tomorrow.

Sunny skies greeted Scotty as he rose to get ready for school. Unexpectedly returning home after being dismissed early when his teacher had failed to show up, he changed into his old jeans and ran up the hill to find the path to the woods.

The ground under his feet felt spongy from all the rain. Small puddles collected in layers of dead leaves, turning the clear water to tannin. He took a deep breath, smelling organic matter rotting; a contribution to the cycle of life. He soon found himself approaching the path that led up to the rock. He crept slowly, not wanting to scare the fairy. Scotty's eyes scanned the area, coming up empty. Struggling with the handholds in the rock, he pulled himself up, grunting loudly in the silence. *Well*, he thought, *I hope that didn't scare the fairy away.* Scaling the top of the rock, he discovered an empty surface.

Dejectedly, he surveyed the surrounding area from his perch. Reaching into his pocket, he pulled out a plastic-wrapped piece of birthday cake. A bit stale, but he didn't think the fairy would notice. Smoothing out the plastic wrap, he pushed the squashed cake toward the edge of the rock. No, he'd better put the cake closer to him. Standing, he eyeballed the position of the cake. Still not liking it, he stood to move it again, a bit more to the middle. Turning, he glanced at his seat and gasped, doing a double take. There was his fairy, sitting in the spot he'd just vacated.

Thumping down hard on the rock, he stared at the fairy's eyes. They made him dizzy with their pulsing golden rainbows leaving him speechless and mesmerized. Neither one moved.

"Are you a fairy?" Scotty finally demanded an answer, getting no response. "The fairies in my fairy book don't have tails. How come you do?" He felt pressure, his mind filling with a strange aura. He stared at the fairy, who just stared back.

"I am an Oolahan." Scotty heard the words whispered in his mind, the aura bright with color.

"Did you say your name was Lula?" Scotty wondered why the creature, um Lula, hadn't moved its mouth. He'd heard it speak quite clearly. The aura and colors had formed mind words; weird.

"Do I get a wish?"

"What do you mean, young Brother?"

"My wish, everyone gets a wish from a fairy." Scotty grew agitated. If everyone got a wish from a fairy, he wanted to make sure he got his before it disappeared again.

"Brother, I do not have a wish for you. I am here for a mission. I have chosen you. You will be The One."

Huh? The boy scratched his head. He stared at Lula. "I want to pet you, Lula." Standing, Scotty walked toward his new friend.

Walking past the cake, he bent down to pick it up to give to Lula. Being the clumsy little boy he was, he tripped. Caught off balance, he crashed down, head first, rolling near the edge. Dazed, he sat up, perilously close to the drop. Still maintaining a hold on his gift to Lula, he stepped back and fell straight over the edge, landing in a broken heap on the sharp pile of rocks at the base.

The Oolahan scurried over to the edge and looked down. She saw blood, lots of blood. The boy's head sat at an unnatural angle, but she could tell he still lived. Unbidden, her tail shot up in the air, directed down at the boy. The air filled with pressure and the smell of sulfur as her tail extruded its membrane to do its miraculous work.

Unfortunately, the meeting had failed to produce the results she'd hoped for. The unexpected disaster had changed everything. Sighing, the creature spun her head in frustration, trying to contain her disappointment. Lamenting the frailty of human offspring, she realized her mission must wait. Even though the boy had appeared to be a good choice, at the moment his youth disqualified him. She should measure her expectations carefully next time. Remembering the young of humans took twenty two years for their brains to mature, her mistake shamed her.

Life worked more efficiently for her species as all young were born with their birth parent's genetic memory. The fact that humans had not evolved this necessary trait was a severe disadvantage. She'd love to know what the Elders had thought they were accomplishing when they'd handicapped this life form. A simple adjustment to their enzymes during evolution would have turned the trait on. She knew the Elders rarely made mistakes. Perhaps they'd done it deliberately. She promised herself to ask the Womb.

Now, forced to rectify the situation the only way she knew, even though it might cause more problems, she must leave the boy alone. Sadly, she climbed down the rock, wobbling over to the boy. She watched his eyes flutter, bringing him back to consciousness. Hurrying, she reached out to grab the cake, still remarkably intact, clutching it tightly under her arm. She wobbled over to the cairn of rocks that marked the way to the Hive and disappeared.

*

Scotty sat up slowly. *What am I doing on the ground?* He could feel the rough edges of the cold rocks digging into his tender skin. He picked himself up off the chilly rocks and made his way back to the glen he usually played in. Looking around, confusion made him dizzy. Shaking it off, he stretched and yawned, freakishly feeling vigorous. Deciding to return home, he wondered if Abby was back from the doctors. She was so tired of late and he needed to help move Mom's stuff from her bedroom to get ready for the Diaz family. Trudging back down the hill, he wondered what had happened to the piece of birthday cake he'd taken into the woods with him.

Deep inside the cavern, the creature blinked her golden eyes, curled up in her chamber, golden tail wrapped protectively around her furry body as she contemplated the shrinking piece of cake in front of her. She didn't take it to eat, not having that capability. Curiosity compelled her; it had belonged to the human Brother. Maybe it would help with the sadness she felt, knowing he could have been The One. The only reason the Womb had allowed the healing was because she'd caused the incident. The humane solution called for the creature to have let him die in the fall. Sadly, even though he now lived, the human would confront a troublesome road.

She ached with the knowledge that the only thing she envisioned for herself was the unremitting loneliness of passing years. Reaching out with one of her long golden leathery fingers, she stroked the tiny piece of cake and closed her eyes.

You can read more by going to Amazon or Barnes and Noble and clicking on Echo, Species Intervention Book 2.

To You, My Dear Reader,

I want you all to know how heartfelt my appreciation is that you have taken the time to read my books. Being an author is one of the most torturous professions out there and many of us live on the thanks of our readers alone. If anyone cares to leave me an honest review on Amazon.com, Goodreads.com, Smashwords.com, Kobo.com or Barnes and Noble, I would be ever so grateful. You can leave a review on Barnes and Noble and Goodreads without having made the purchase there. Some of you are unaware that Amazon, in particular, promotes books based on the amount of reviews a book gets. No reviews . . . the book will stay a secret.

Don't be afraid to make suggestions or criticize the writing. How else is one to improve? I look forward to your comments!

Yours,
J. K. Accinni

Author's Page

J. K. Accinni was born and raised in Sussex County before moving to Randolph, New Jersey, where she lived with her husband, five dogs and eight rabbits, all rescued. She currently resides in Sarasota, Florida. Mrs. Accinni's passion for wildlife conservation has led her all over the world, including three trips to Africa, where ten years ago, she and her husband fell in love with a baby elephant named Wendi who had been rescued by a wildlife group. That baby is the inspiration for the character Tobi, the elephant featured in her fourth book titled *Hive*.

The character of Caesar is inspired by a real life iconic tiger from Big Cat Habitat and Gulf Coast Sanctuary in Sarasota. A portion of the proceeds from her third book, *Armageddon Cometh*, will be donated to the sanctuary in support of the enormous expense required to house and feed the displaced wildlife in their care. Mrs. Accinni invites her readers to visit *bigcathabitat.org* to view the astounding facility and plan a visit with your family.

Mrs. Accinni also invites you to visit her webpage at www.SpeciesIntervention.com, where information on The Big Cat Habitat and Gulf Coast Sanctuary can also be viewed. Readers are encouraged to comment about the book or your own creature experiences.